YOURS
IN THE BOND

Rashid Darden

Old Gold Soul   Washington, DC

Old Gold Soul

www.oldgoldsoul.com | www.rashiddarden.com

Yours in the Bond is a work of fiction. Any references to real people, events, establishments, organizations, or locales are intended to give the fiction a sense of reality and authenticity. Other names, characters, and incidents are either the product of the author's imagination or are used fictitiously.

First Edition

Cover Design by Boogie Pittrell: www.helloboogie.com

ISBN: 978-0-9765986-7-1

For my brothers.

Acknowledgements

My thanks always to God.

Thank you to Tony Burks, Cerrice Dawson, Michael Goulet, Jeff Marcella, Geoff Riggins, Muhammad Salaam, Maxine Sharp, Tom Southard, and Katherine Steadwell.

Gratitude, always, to Tiana Beard, Josh Blount, Nikki Butler, Zoila Primo, Tara Proctor, and Neil Wade.

Special thanks to the town of Conway, North Carolina, where I completed the first draft of this novel on Christmas Day 2017.

And my thanks always to my blood family, including my mother Carolyn Darden-Stutely; and my fraternal families: The Alphas, The Freemasons, The Apollonians, APO, and GXP.

The Beginning:
Charlotte, North Carolina
Summer 2001

I woke up. He sat on the edge of the bed in his wrinkled white t-shirt. He checked his phone, tossed it lightly to the bed, sniffed, and stood up. He stretched his arms over his head and farted. He scratched his scalp through his voluminous afro.

Such a boy, I thought.

I studied him.

Rather than sit upright in bed, I lay there, enveloped by the white comforter and down pillows. I studied him, undetected. He took off his white t-shirt and stared at himself in the mirror for a few moments. From my vantage point I saw a wrestler's build: broad shoulders, a muscular back, a thin waist, a juicy behind covered by navy blue boxer briefs, and thick thighs.

He placed his thumbs in the band of his underwear and bent over, coming quickly out of them. He left them in a pile with his t-shirt and walked to the bathroom, his substantial genitalia bouncing casually in front of him.

The door closed. A faint metallic screech was followed by the whoosh of water from the shower.

I grabbed my erection and closed my eyes tight while I replayed the vision of his ass and dick over and over. In my ears, I heard his hearty laugh, his corny jokes, and his gravelly whisper. This man was my everything and he didn't even know it.

I looked at the clock radio on the nightstand.

5:47pm.

The closing banquet would start in about an hour. I released my grip on my penis and finally separated myself from the magnetic attraction of the most comfortable bed I'd ever slept in. I stood up, walked bare-chested and boxer shorted to the closet, and pulled out the ironing board and iron. The whine of the ironing board opening pierced the room's silence. The iron began to warm, then hiss shortly after I plugged it in. Walking back to the closet, I grabbed my suit as well as his.

Our souvenirs and ephemera from the Beta Chi Phi Leadership Conference got intermingled on the dresser alongside my camera, which I'd barely used. Name tags and snacks and agendas and handouts all fought each other for space. I did my best to separate them as the iron got hot.

Brother Eustace Dailey
Beta Chapter
Harvard/Tufts/MIT

My paper nametag was in a simple, burgundy holder on a lanyard. Underneath the rectangle with my identifying information was a small gold pennant identifying my special status: *Neophyte*.

His nametag was similar:

Brother Jeremy J. Carter
Alpha Chapter
Boston University/Boston College

But the pennant beneath said *National Board of Directors*.

He began mumbling in the shower while I began ironing. These past few days had been…

"Fellas! If yo bitch wanna get buck wild! Just go back and smoke black and milds!"

"Those ain't the words!" I shouted through the bathroom door.

"They are today!" JJ shouted back. He continued to stumble his way through the song while he got clean.

His suit and shirt were pressed, and I laid them out on the other bed in the room. I then focused on my own suit. Our third roommate for the past few days was already dressed and out of the room. He was the National Second Vice President, a position earmarked for collegians, like JJ's Undergraduate Member-at-Large spot. He was no doubt at one of many receptions or meetings which required his attendance over the past few days.

His absence didn't bother me. I was keen on having as much one-on-one time with JJ as possible, and he seemed just as eager.

My chapter wasn't terribly interested in attending the biannual leadership conference, preferring instead to attend *en masse* the National Convention in even numbered years. When my dean of pledges heard I'd like to attend, he quickly made the call across town to Alpha Chapter, and ultimately JJ, who welcomed me to join his room, where his colleague on the board would also be joining us.

My chapter paid for my conference registration. All I had to do was get a flight from my home in St. Louis to Charlotte.

JJ emerged from the bathroom with a white towel wrapped around his waist. Droplets of water dotted both his body and his afro. He looked at me, then the ironing board.

"Yo…you ironed my suit?" he asked

"It was right there. You were in the shower. It didn't kill me."

"Thanks, bro," he said with a smile. I shrugged.

"It's nothing."

He reached past me and opened the dresser drawer. He grabbed his trimmers, black socks, and black underwear. He returned to the bathroom but left the door open as he began to shave.

"We don't have a lot of time. You need to shower?"

"Yeah…I do. Do you mind?"

"Mm-mm," he said. He held his upper lip in place while he shaped up his moustache. I took off my underwear. He stole a glance at me before he turned his attention back to his facial hair.

The hot water rushing over me competed with the loud buzz of the trimmers. The shower curtain was transparent at the top and opaque from my shoulders down. I washed my body while JJ meticulously shaved, picked at blemishes, and moisturized his skin.

I wanted to relieve myself badly, but I couldn't. For the past three intense days I had sat with this man in training workshops, fallen asleep with this man on shuttle buses, drank liquor with this man to the point of nearly passing out, and talked with him like I've never talked to anyone else.

The glances. The touches on the shoulder. The hugs. It became overwhelming. And despite what I already knew about his sexual orientation, I fell for him.

Hard.

I hadn't felt for somebody like this in years, and while I hoped the feeling would never end, I also wanted it to end—needed it to end—so I could go back to the life I was supposed to be living.

In the main room, as we got dressed, he cut through our silence.

"Eustace. Can I ask you something?"

"Sure." I tucked in my shirt.

"You think I'm attractive?" JJ asked.

"Of course, I do," I answered a little too quickly. His eyebrows rose, and my heart raced.

"Of course?" he repeated.

"You're handsome," I affirmed. "You don't strike me as the kind of guy who needs reminding."

"I don't, according to Sylvia."

"Yes, Sylvia. Of course."

"My girlfriend." His countenance changed. Deflated, almost.

"I know. I've seen her around."

"Yeah. Sometimes you find yourself in situations…"

"Relationships?"

"Yeah…relationships. After a while, it's just weird. You look at this person when you wake up and you think 'I guess I'll spend the rest of my life with them.' And it's a weird feeling. Everything falls into place. But you don't necessarily feel that thing you're supposed to feel. That little bit of extra."

"Are you happy?" I asked.

"I'm happy. My folks love Sylvia. She fits with what I'm trying to do. I like spending time with her. And she got good pussy."

I giggled.

"You ain't never had no pussy, have you?" he asked.

"Ew, no!"

"You say it like getting pussy ain't normal!"

"It ain't…for me. Hey, if that's what you like, more power to you, man."

"I do like it. You really never tried it?"

"Naw."

"Then how you know you really gay?"

"Are you for real?"

"Absolutely. Seems like if you never tried it, you won't know for sure."

"JJ…being gay isn't about not putting my dick in a vagina. I could do that if I wanted to. It doesn't appeal to me, but I could do it. Being gay means that I love men. I love the way we move. The way we laugh. Our strength. Our vulnerability. I love that, man. I can be myself in the arms of a man. Just like you can be yourself in Sylvia's arms."

"Damn. You're really poetic."

"I don't know, it just happens sometimes." Struggling with my necktie, I gave up and tried to tie it again

"You think that's normal, to feel all those things? I mean, gay or straight," he asked.

"It's normal for me. I think when you love somebody, you should feel more like yourself. No pretense. No show. Just realness."

"It should feel like that." JJ nodded. I swallowed.

"If it doesn't...maybe..."

"If it doesn't, then maybe it will," he interrupted. I nodded.

"Hopefully it will." I continued struggling with my necktie. This time, the knot was way too big.

"Here, let me," JJ offered. I put my hands at my side and raised my chin while he worked.

"Why does it...why did you want to know if I found you attractive? I mean, what difference does it make, right? It's not like..."

"I just...I never had a gay friend. And spending these past few days with you, I just...I feel like we're going to be friends for a long time. I just wanted to know what you really thought about me."

"You think we're cool because I'm attracted to you?" I asked.

"No. Not that it would be terrible if you were. Or weren't. I don't know. Just ignore me."

He smiled and finished tying my tie.

"Perfect," he announced. I looked at myself in the mirror. His hand lingered on my chest.

"JJ, what are we doing?" I asked.

"I want to know everything about you. These past few days..."

"These past few days," I echoed.

"They've been...everything."

"Complicated."

"Perfect."

"Surreal."

"I want to know everything. I want to know what it was like when you first...you know."

"No, I don't."

"Why you being so difficult? What was your first time like with a man?"

"My first time? My very first time? JJ, I don't know. It was cool."

"Cool?"

"Yeah...cool. I really liked him. He was versatile, so we tried a little of everything."

"Everything? Even...anal?" he whispered.

"Yeah. Even anal."

"Did you like it?"

"I like giving a lot. Receiving? Depends on the guy. He's got to take his time. I don't do that casually, though."

"How old were you the first time?"

"17."

"When's the last time you were with a dude?"

"The last ti—JJ, really?"

"I told you--I don't have any gay friends, man. I'm sorry."

"No. It's okay. I was last with a dude...the week after I crossed."

"Boyfriend?"

"Nah. I haven't had a boyfriend since I was in high school. And he was the only one I've had."

"Really? All these gay dudes in Boston and you ain't found one of your own?"

I shrugged.

"I'm not looking too hard, I guess. I'll find a dude on BlackPlanet or CollegeClub, but that's just for fun. None of them really do much for me outside of the physical."

"You seem pretty cool. You could find a dude if you wanted to."

"Thanks. It would be nice to have something like what you and Sylvia have."

He forced a smile, which relaxed after a few moments. He turned away.

"Uh oh...sore subject."

"Sylvia's everything I could ask for."

"But?"

"Nothing. She's everything I could ask for. I want that for everybody."

I nodded.

"Eustace, I...I really enjoyed hanging out with you at this conference." He faced me once more.

"So did I. Hanging out with you. We'll have plenty of memories to tell our kids, right?"

He smiled and touched my arm. His look became serious. My heart raced again, and I began to float twenty, thirty, forty years into my future, knowing this was it—the moment—the instant in which everything would change. Two men in suits and burgundy and gold ties touched, and nothing would be the same.

JJ looked up sharply. A rustle at the door got his attention: the sound of a hotel key card being inserted into its slot. With a faint beep, the door unlocked, and the knob turned. I exhaled, annoyed, yet relieved that my life hadn't changed in that moment after all.

Our lean fraternity brother and roommate for the conference, Adrian Collins, entered the room with a smile. He was our Brother from Sigma Chapter, chartered at both Potomac University and Rock Creek College in Washington, DC.

"What are you smiling about?" JJ sneered.

"After this dry ass banquet, our terms will be officially halfway over!"

I laughed as Adrian and JJ dapped each other up.

"You mean being National Second Vice President and Undergraduate Member-at-Large aren't everything you dreamed?" I asked sarcastically.

Adrian closed his eyes and slowly shook his head.

"The board meetings are like…the worst chapter meeting you've ever been to. Except everybody's old," Adrian said.

"Old and drunk," JJ added. "Which is actually pretty entertaining."

"Are y'all ready, though?" Adrian asked.

"Yeah. Pretty much," JJ said while slipping on his shoes.

"You got your camera?" Adrian asked me.

"Getting it now." I slid the small digital point-and-shoot into my jacket pocket.

"Then let's go. Leadership Conference 2001 is officially over," Adrian said.

"Let brotherly love continue," JJ and I said in unison. We looked at each other and smiled. Adrian chuckled, turned, and exited the room first. JJ touched my back, guiding me to the door. My back muscles tensed. His hand lingered for another second, then slowly slid away.

We walked quickly down the carpeted hallway, arriving at the elevator in no time. Adrian quickly pushed the button and stood back. A soft tone signaled the lift's arrival and we boarded.

The reflection of us in the mirrored elevator doors showed three men in black suits, burgundy and gold neckties, and gold fraternity pins. JJ was the shortest of the three of us but appeared to be the oldest. His usual look of vague annoyance made us question whether he was having a good day or not. Adrian, in contrast, had a natural smile about him, as though he was in on a secret that something wonderful was about to happen.

JJ and Adrian wore fraternity pins encircled with red stones, signifying that they were members of the National Board of Directors. My pin was plain. I was a regular member—a neophyte who had crossed the previous spring and got lucky enough to befriend the two most powerful collegians in Beta right before they became alumni.

I was the tallest of the trio. The tallest, the darkest, and at times, the quietest. There were times when I could trade barbs with the best of them—and Adrian and JJ were the best of them—but there were times when I sat and listened as a neo should.

In the reflection, I noticed JJ turn his head slightly toward me. I looked back at him. A smile threatened to pull the corners of my mouth back. JJ grinned—unrestrained—then quickly looked at the floor. I looked away, trying to maintain my composure. I looked at our reflection a second time and noticed Adrian's one raised eyebrow looking back at me. I couldn't tell if his face expressed surprise, disapproval, or tacit endorsement of whatever was happening.

Perhaps it was all three.

The elevator doors slid open to the hotel lobby, which was already filled with brothers in their dark suits and tuxedoes, waiting for the banquet to start. It felt as though all eyes were instantly on us.

The convention photographer came out of nowhere.

"Hey! Can I get a picture of the undergraduate board members?"

"Only if Brother Dailey is in the photo with us," JJ demanded.

"Who's Brother Dailey?" the photographer asked. JJ looked at me and waited for me to introduce myself.

"Oh…I am." I waved slightly.

Adrian and JJ flanked me. Adrian's hand found its way to my shoulder while JJ grabbed my side.

"This the holy trinity of Beta right here. Y'all just don't know," JJ announced. The three of us laughed while the shutter clicked on the camera.

"Now, a few with the sign," Adrian instructed. I crossed my arms and held the "Keys of Brotherhood" hand sign while JJ and Adrian did the same. More shutter clicks.

My favorite outtakes from that shoot were images of the three of us laughing: Adrian, with his head thrown back and eyes closed, without a care in the world; me, all teeth, looking downward to the floor; and JJ, looking at me with a closed-mouth smile.

Over the years, there would be many more days and nights like this, and the pattern was always the same: Adrian was the care-free one. I was the unsure one. And no matter where we were in the world, or in life, Jeremy Jacob Carter always had his eyes on me.

Part One:
Willemstad, Curacao
Summer 2003

Weddings and funerals. Days that new families begin and days that families say goodbye. Here, on this verdant hilltop overlooking a Curacao beach, a new family was beginning, officially, in front of God, family, and friends who are family. Here, man and man would be joined as one in the culmination of a love story that, to all of us, seemed epic and revolutionary, but now, perhaps is as ordinary as any other love.

On this day, my fraternity brother Adrian Collins married his soul mate, professional basketball player Isaiah Aiken. The guest list was exclusive, yet the audience of well-wishers seemed far more populous than the fifty or so who had made the trek from the states to this tropical hideaway in the Caribbean Sea. Adrian and Isaiah were the kind of people who could make fifty people seem like 500 in their exuberance.

I sat to the rear so that I could see every little detail. Although Adrian had not asked me to be the official photographer, he did ask me to bring my "good" camera, just in case. He told me that he knew I would catch things that their hired photographer would not, because I knew the couple so well already.

As I discreetly took photos from my corner seat, I couldn't help but become overwhelmed by Adrian and Isaiah's beauty. Beautiful is not a word I would ordinarily use to describe men, but there is no word more apt. Perhaps it was the rich blues of the sky, or the pure white clouds. Maybe it was the lush, green lawn, or maybe even the sharp angles of their haircuts next to the broad curves of their shoulders and biceps barely contained by their tuxedo jackets. Whatever it was, I was enthralled. Enchanted.

What added to the joy of this moment was that their curly-topped son, Zion Aiken, shared this moment with them. Zion was Isaiah's biological child by a previous relationship and now lived with them full-time in Brooklyn, as Isaiah's professional team was anchored there.

These men, my fraternity brother and his groom, beamed with love, with pride, with admiration for each other. As they recited vows and exchanged rings, tears of joy freely fell from their eyes. Their mothers could be heard sniffling from the front row. It was a day that I was most proud to be a black gay man.

The couple was flanked by their closest friends and relatives. On Isaiah's side were cousins and basketball teammates, including Hodari Hudgins, who played for the Washington team. As straight as he might have been, even he was fraught with emotion at the sight of his friends making it official.

On Adrian's side stood his best friend Nina Bradley, a tall and beautiful brown-skinned woman with short dreadlocks. Next to her stood five of our fraternity brothers: Adrian's Dean and Big Brother Steven Jones, himself a newlywed; Adrian's Little Brother Christopher White; Adrian's line Brother Mohammed Bilal, back in the states studying for a PhD in history; and the freshly clean-shaven Jeremy Jacob Carter, fast friends since their stint on the national board. Rounding out Adrian's side was one of his best friends, another line brother named Calen Hawkins. He was a gargantuan professional football player, wide and tall like a brick house. He was a stark contrast to the lean basketball players on the other side of the aisle.

The brotherhood on display during the ceremony was the stuff that pledge sessions were made of. Someday, each man on that altar would tell a new group of pledges how meaningful it was to stand there on behalf of one of their own, even in a gay wedding before gay marriages were legal in all the United States.

I had known Adrian for two years by then. Although we had become good friends, I felt out of place being included in the celebration. I was a baby in the fraternity and an outsider to Sigma Chapter in DC.

I'd pledged while a Sophomore at Harvard through the Beta Chapter, also known as the Soul of Beta Chi Phi. I went over in 2001, the same semester that Adrian and JJ had graduated from Potomac and Boston University, respectively. Despite being two years ahead of me, they looked out for me as though I were their own flesh and blood.

So even though I questioned why I was invited, I knew why I was invited. They know me. They're my brothers. Beta is small. Beta is elite. And fundamentally, all Betas know each other.

"...you may now seal this union with a kiss!" the preacher exclaimed at ceremony's end.

Isaiah took Adrian's face in his hands and planted the softest, sweetest kiss upon his lips. Adrian wrapped his arms around his husband's neck and got on his tiptoes to kiss him back.

The audience cooed, cheered, and applauded. Adrian and Isaiah were finally together. Officially.

They strode back down the aisle, smiling and waving to their well-wishers.

They passed by me in the final rows. Isaiah pointed and smiled excitedly. Adrian said "Hey!" and in that moment, I snapped my favorite picture of the day.

JJ sauntered behind them and smiled at me, too. I smiled back and looked to the ground at my shiny oxfords.

We moved inside the resort to a gorgeous ballroom decorated entirely in white with accents of gold. It was an old, stone room with floor to ceiling doors that led back out toward the beach.

I was soon spirited away by an usher who led me to my table. I wasn't sure whether the precise orchestration of the ceremony and reception was the work of Adrian's attention to detail or Isaiah's desire to have everything perfect for the love of his life. But I was sure Adrian had something to do with how the seating worked out—it was clear that we were at tables with people who Adrian thought we should know better. And if all else failed, at least we had one person we knew.

I sat next to JJ, who was as happy to see me as I was to see him. I'd first truly interacted with him when I was a pledge at Harvard. He was the most hardcore, meanest Big Brother in New England, with a face fixed in a perpetual accusatory sneer. His impossibly symmetrical afro crowned his head, adding inches to his modest height. He might have been too tall for a Napoleon complex, but he was certainly that big brother who none of us from Beta Chapter wanted to see.

Given his status as a senior when I pledged, he was on somewhat of a farewell tour among the pledges in our area. I had seen him around before I pledged and thought I would hate him, just from how he looked. And he didn't disappoint when he finally met the pledges. What a dick.

Did I mention he was Alpha Chapter? No, not *from* Alpha Chapter. He was, is, and always would *be* Alpha Chapter, the home of our beloved fraternity, the chapter from which all other chapters sprang forth. Mighty Alpha Chapter. Amazing Alpha Chapter. Established in 1970 and all you other chapters could *never*.

Yes, Big Brother Jeremy Jacob Carter was Alpha Chapter, and don't you ever forget it.

Despite his Alpha Arrogance and Alpha Aggression, Big Brother Jeremy was beloved by the brothers of Beta Chapter in Cambridge. He had, the previous year, been elected to national office in the fraternity. We had a national second vice-president to represent the undergraduates—that was Adrian Collins. We also had two undergraduate members at large, and Jeremy was one of those. The other was a brother from down south, but we never saw him. We knew that Big Brother Jeremy Jacob Carter was supposed to be our pride and joy because he was from our home district.

And don't you forget *that*, either.

"Fancy meeting you here," he said as he sat next to me.

"Good to see you, bro." I rose to embrace him and give him the fraternal handshake.

"Beautiful wedding," I added as we sat.

"Awesome. Not a dry eye in the house, huh?"

"Not a one." I looked into my glass of water. "You looked good up there."

He looked at his lap, his smile going strong.

"Thank you," he said softly.

"Yaaaassss! She is at the second-best table of the evening!" a golden voiced woman said.

Nina Bradley and Hodari Hudgins took their places at our table. We rose briefly, and sat back down again. She looked as lovely as I'd ever seen her and Hodari looked equally as handsome.

"She who?" JJ asked.

"She who?" Nina echoed. "She, me, her, we're all here so let the party start!" Hodari laughed heartily.

"Is she referring to herself in the third person?" JJ whispered.

"She's probably already drunk," I laughed.

The rest of the table was filled with other Betas, basketball players, and family members. Adrian and Isaiah were certain to make sure the wedding party was spread out among all the guest tables rather than ensconced among themselves. What a smart idea. What a great gift to me, at least.

"Ladies and gentlemen, Mr. Adrian Collins and Mr. Isaiah Aiken."

The men of the hour walked into the ballroom hand in hand.

"We just want to thank all of you for coming out to celebrate our special day with us," Adrian said.

"We love you all very much and we could not have made it as a couple…as partners…and now as husbands without your love and support," Isaiah added.

"We might be in Curacao, but consider yourselves at home," Adrian said.

"Eat until you're stuffed. Drink as much as you can stand. Love as much as you want…all night long," Isaiah said.

"Make a new friend. This weekend is all about love. Drink up!"

The room erupted with applause and cheers. JJ stood and I soon followed. Before long, the entire room cheered the new couple.

Dinner was sumptuous: Bacon-wrapped scallops, Caesar salad, angel hair pasta, steak and salmon, wedding cupcakes.

The drinks never stopped flowing, not even for a second. JJ kept returning to the table with cocktails for the both of us. Neither of us had yet learned the beauty in moderation.

Adrian's little brother Christopher went out to the dance floor as the ambient music lowered.

"Calling all Brothers, to the floor!" he sang slowly.

"Ooooh, Beta!" we all replied.

"We got one here, but we need some more!"

"Ooooh, Beta!"

All the Betas in the room continued our song that beckoned Betas one and all to our circle. I leaned over to JJ in between verses.

"Oh my God, JJ. The room is spinning. How we gonna sing this sweetheart song?" I asked.

"I don't know. But we gon' do it."

I was easily a good four or five inches taller than JJ, but somehow he helped me stand and kept me upright as we walked to the dance floor, answering the call.

We assembled our circle and began slowly singing our sweetheart song in unison.

There comes a time in every Beta's life
A time to settle on down
To find somebody that won't cause you strife
And you know that he'll always be around

So tell me, my Brother, tell me true
What is it that you're gonna do?

Adrian, who had been silently standing next to his father through the song, broke away from the circle and entered it. He sang in a resplendent tenor with all his heart:

Brothers, I…choose him.
Brothers, I…want him.
Brothers, I…need him.
Brothers, I…love him.

Adrian reached back toward his opening in the circle and stretched his arm out to Isaiah, who had turned beet red. The audience collectively cried out in approval as Isaiah walked to the middle of the circle.

We continued as we closed the circle back.

There comes a time in every Beta's life
A time to settle on down
We welcome you to our noble family
And you know that we'll always be around
And you know that we'll always be around
And you know that we'll always be…around

Adrian kissed Isaiah. The audience exploded with applause and we in the circle joined them.

"Beeeeee-Chi!" called JJ.

"Chiiiiiii-Phi!" we responded.

The audience politely clapped as we began to disperse, but the DJ began to play what we considered our unofficial national song: Zapp and Roger's "So Ruff So Tuff."

We went nuts on the dance floor, quickly forming a line. The older Bros stood to the back. Sigma Chapter's step master, curly-haired Ciprian Williams, was at the beginning of the line and Adrian stood right behind him. We paid attention to the cues, and somehow, even in all our drunkenness, we stayed on beat for much of the song. As we rounded the curve, I saw that the younger brothers were doing our double-time stroll, hopping about on the ones, the twos, the threes, and the fours. Meanwhile, the elder brothers, led by Adrian's dad, brought up the rear with one of their old-school walks. Rather than bopping around the dance floor, they merely strolled along—slowly, but on the beat. No matter how much energy we had, we'd always be shown up by smooth old geezers.

I took a break to head to the restroom after we were finished strolling. When I returned to the table, JJ was in the middle of a conversation with one of Isaiah's female cousins, a brown-skinned, curvy beauty with cornrows leading to an afro puff.

"So...like...is this even a legal ceremony?" she asked.

"I mean it's not legal-legal, but you know Isaiah and Adrian got lawyers up the ass, so they're doing what they can."

"The Curacao cops ain't finna jump in this bitch, are they?"

"Naw, Isaiah got the entire damn perimeter blocked off and the cops got paid off not to bother us—so I heard."

"That's what's up. Are you here by yourself?" she asked.

"Not exactly," JJ said. He looked at me and looked back at the cousin.

"Oh, are y'all...?"

"Us? No. We're not together. That's my boy, though."

"I mean, you know, had to ask. This is my first gay wedding and I'm turned all upside down."

"I feel you. I...I have a girl back home. She was invited, but she doesn't..."

I rolled my eyes.

"Uh oh, it's some drama?" the cousin asked. JJ laughed.

"She's still getting used to the fact that I'm as liberal as I am, that's all. She's pretty religious."

"Well she gonna have to get over all that. It's a new day!"

"Indeed it is," JJ said. He looked at me and touched my shoulder.

"Is it?" I asked him with a smile. He stared back at me in silence until we both collapsed in laughter.

"Mmm-hmm," the cousin said as she sipped her cocktail.

"What?" JJ asked.

"Nothing."

"What?!" JJ insisted.

"Y'all go together," she knowingly.

"Go to—we do not!" JJ said incredulously.

"Yeah. Okay."

"I'm straight, I swear to God."

The cousin continued to sip her cocktail and slowly rose.

"It was nice meeting you, JJ. Eustace. I'll see you on the dance floor."

She sashayed away, bobbing her head to the beat of one of Rod Lee's best Baltimore Club mixes.

"You see that shit?" JJ asked. All I could do is laugh.

"Whatchu laughing at?" JJ asked.

"I'm gonna go dance. You can stay here and be mad if you wanna."

I staggered as best I could to the dance floor, content to dance by myself if I had to. The room swam with people in love with life. I found Isaiah's cousin, grabbed her hand, and asked if I could dance with her. She obliged.

"Your little friend not gonna get mad?" she asked as she began to roll her hips.

"My little friend," I repeated with a laugh and an eye roll.

"He'll be your man. Watch." I laughed again, closed my eyes, and shook my head. I rolled my hips in time with hers, grabbing her around the waist as the Baltimore club dissolved into DC go-go.

"Awww shit!" she exclaimed.

"I love the east coast," I sighed. I closed my eyes and let the music take over. This was the best party I'd ever been to, and I'd been to Chocolate City at MIT on more than a few occasions.

I glanced over at Adrian and Isaiah who were having the time of their lives. Isaiah, as tall as he was, somehow managed to back that thang up against Adrian, whose face was serious and sweaty. Isaiah popped and rolled while Adrian struggled to maintain control. It was hilarious and adorable at the same time.

Isaiah's mom joined her niece and I on the dance floor. I toasted her. She smiled and quickly kissed me on the cheek. All love.

I lost all track of time until Nina, Adrian, Isaiah, and I were the sole survivors on the dance floor. JJ returned with a glass of water.

"Where you been?" I asked.

"Chillin'. Drink this."

"Thank you," I said.

"Hey. Let's get out of here."

"That sounds like a plan." I gave JJ dap, then walked over to Adrian and Isaiah.

"I know this is your night. But this was probably the best night of my life, too. Thank you. For being you."

"Aww, baby bro. Thank you for coming," Adrian said.

"We love you so much, Eustace. Thank you for being here," Isaiah added.

"I love you guys, too," I smiled. They brought me into a group embrace. JJ, too, said his farewells, and we were off to walk the 500 or so feet to the resort's guest rooms.

The rooms were down a stone pathway lined with palm trees and interspersed with lampposts and benches. I struggled to stay on the path.

"Walk straight, nigga!" JJ barked.

"I am walking straight," I said.

"On what planet?" We took a right turn toward my room.

"You gonna stop talking to me like I'm a pledge, though."

"You always gonna be my pledge. Spit my founders, quick!"

I dropped my room key to the ground outside my door and placed my fists against my chest.

"Alvaro Luis Castillo! Steven Russell Harris! Jonathan Thomas Jackson! Lamont Tyson! William Lucas Wade!"

"Nigga if you don't get us into this room!" JJ laughed.

"Don't challenge my knowledge, homes. You know how Beta Chapter rolls," I said smugly. I opened the door to my room and turned on a lamp.

"Oh, I know. But don't forget who taught you the real history of Beta Chapter." JJ peeled off his jacket and threw it into the plush, salmon colored chair in the corner. I unloosed my tie.

"Everybody knows why we're called the Soul of Beta Chi Phi. We all take that trip to Brother Dawkins' grave when we're pledging."

He turned around and crossed his arms.

"Why you acting like that?" he asked.

"Like what? We've been doing this long as we've known each other," I said.

"What?"

"This back and forth."

"Man…" JJ let his sentence trail off. He rubbed the back of his naked head.

"Rest in peace, afro," I said.

"Sometimes I think I still have it. Phantom fro."

I smiled and looked away from him. I'd forgotten that my camera was slung over my shoulder. I carefully took it off and turned it on.

"Wow, I took a couple hundred pictures, man."

"A couple hundred? Damn."

I walked over to my bed and sat on the pure white sheets. I recounted every moment of that day through the images I'd captured. I smiled, laughed, and tilted my head trying to figure out how I'd taken such good photos despite not remembering the ones toward the end.

"Can I see?" JJ asked. He had come out of his shirt and sat in his white undershirt. His brown biceps bulged out from under his short sleeves.

"Sure. Just hit this button to move forward." I passed him the camera and he carefully held it in his hands.

While he scrolled through, I turned my back to him and began peeling out of my suit. Curacao was hot and it was time to take off these layers.

"These are good, my man," JJ said.

"Thank you."

"You're welcome. You should consider doing more with your photography. I bet you could make a full-time job out of it."

"I don't know, JJ. I just be taking pictures."

"Yeah, I know. But still…if you ever get tired of management consulting, I truly don't think you'll have any worries."

I smiled. I was in my t-shirt and underwear now, rummaging through my suitcase to find a pair of shorts.

"Did I tell you how happy I was that we'll be in DC together?" he asked.

"Yep." Finally, found my crimson Harvard shorts. I slid them on and climbed back on the bed. I reclined on the pile of pillows at the head.

"I kinda wish we were living together. Don't make no sense to…"

"I already told you, JJ. Not gonna happen."

"Spoilsport," he said.

"You're in a good mood."

JJ carefully put my camera on the table near the big comfy chair. He stood up, walked over to the lamp, and turned it off. In the dark, I saw him slide out of his suit pants and carelessly leave them in a clump on the floor.

"Good mood is an understatement," he announced. In an instant, he climbed onto the bed and crawled next to me. He laid on his stomach, gazing at me while he rested his chin on his folded arms.

"This just might be the most fun I've ever had," he said.

"Me too."

JJ sniffed the air, his nose scrunching into a wrinkled brown dot.

"Is that you?" he asked.

"What happened? I stink?"

"Not at all. Your cologne last this long?"

"I guess so."

JJ smirked and crawled closer to me, raising himself into a push-up position and lowering his head next to my neck. He leaned his face close and inhaled deeply.

"Yeah, you smell good," he said, looking down at me. His arms gave out against his weight and he collapsed, falling half on my body and half on the bed. We laughed.

"Get your drunk ass off me," I said.

"Naw man," he laughed.

"You're so wasted."

"So are you."

Without a care, I ran my hand over JJ's bald head. He exhaled slowly and closed his eyes.

"Don't stop."

He wrapped his arms around me and held me tight. I loosened up and hugged him back. In the darkness, we cuddled. My chest heaved as I breathed. His head rose and fell along with me.

"I could stay like this forever," he said.

"Are you coming on to me?" I asked.

"I'm not gay, man."

"You sniffing my neck. You got your arm around me. You letting me stroke your hair. Well, your head."

"You're drunk."

"So are you."

"That wedding man. That was some of the most beautiful shit ever."

"No bullshit."

"I have so much respect for them. In the face of everything, they made it. They really made it. And you know what?"

"What?"

"I respect you, too."

"Thank you, JJ."

"I mean it."

"I know you do."

JJ looked up into my eyes and in an instant kissed me on the cheek.

"It's contagious," he said. "Just being here makes me feel...alive. I don't know what it is. Fresh air. The water. The people. I'm happy. Like there's no other place in this universe that I'd rather be right now than here next to you. Crazy how love is, right?"

"You saying you love me?" I asked. I looked at the ceiling and focused on the miniscule flecks of light that penetrated the drawn curtains.

"Of course I love you. Why is it that we as men get so crazy when it comes to telling each other that we love each other? Yes, I love you. And it didn't take me long to figure out that I did. Charlotte. Day one."

I looked from the ceiling to JJ's eyes.

"I love you, too," I said.

"But don't say it just because I said it, nigga."

"I'm not saying it just because you did. I just...never say it first."

"Never?"

"No."

"For real?"

"Never ever."

"Why not?"

"Because. I don't want to give anybody that sort of power over me. When you tell someone that you love them, and you say it first, that's an invitation for them to own you, to humiliate you, to destroy you. I will never say it first."

"Don't you trust anybody?" JJ asked hopefully.

"I don't trust anyone to *not* hurt me." Damn. This was one of those moments where the smooth thing to say would have been "I trust *you*." But I wasn't wired to be smooth. I was wired to be honest. Moreover, I was built for self-preservation. JJ chipped away at my armor.

"Trust me." JJ commanded.

"You hurt me, too."

"No, I won't."

"JJ, you already are."

"How you figure?"

"What do you think this looks like?"

"Who cares how it looks?"

"Put yourself in my shoes. Imagine that you're in bed with someone that you've always been attracted to—that knows you're attracted to them. They're holding you, telling you they love you... but you know that when this little vacation is over he's going back to his girlfriend."

"I don't want to hurt you, Eustace."

"I know you don't."

"And I'm not gay."

"I know."

"But sometimes you make me wish that I was."

I sighed deeply.

"This is the shit I'm talking about. I'm not spending my life chasing you," I said.

"I don't want you to waste a second chasing me."

He held me tighter. His stubble brushed against my shoulder. His hairy legs rested against mine. I breathed.

"Would you be happy if this is all I could ever give you?" he asked.

"All you do is touch me."

"You the only man I want to touch like this."

I stared at him. He looked at me with a wicked grin. I blinked slowly and turned away from him.

"And you think that's supposed to sustain me?" I scoffed. He slid close to me and wrapped his arms and legs tightly around me.

"It's all I got to give you," he said, hugging me until his face was a pancake against my back.

"You know I love you for real, right?" he continued.

"I know."

"You get me. And I get you. Let's just...let's just be what we are. Whatever we are. Okay?"

What I said next could not be blamed on alcohol. It couldn't be chalked up to youthful indiscretion or a lapse in otherwise good judgment.

I knew what I was doing.

I wanted this man in any way that I could have him, even if it meant the pulsating erection in my underwear would never be satisfied by any part of his body.

When I was with him, all my senses were alive at the same time. All my organs pulsed to the beat of his spirit. I was pulled in all directions when I was with him, and I ached from the tension, but I felt alive—more alive than any other moment.

"Okay," I said.

"Okay?" he repeated. I turned back over to face him one last time.

"Yes. What we have is enough."

I leaned in and kissed his forehead lightly. He closed his eyes, smiled, and held onto me.

My erection never went away, and neither did his, but for what he couldn't or wouldn't satisfy within me with his body, he more than made up for with his unabashed intimacy with me.

I didn't know what would happen on the next day, or the day after that, but for that one night in Curacao, I was satisfied.

Part Two:
Washington,
District of Columbia
Summer and Fall 2005

Chapter One:
Late July 2005

Two years and a hundred lifetimes later, Curacao was little more than a faded memory of a summer camp crush. If I thought too hard about it, it was hard to believe it had ever happened at all.

Although JJ and I both moved to DC within weeks of each other, his adjustment to his first year at Georgetown Law was far more important than any confessions or promises in a dark island bedroom. No, Jeremy Jacob Carter fell into his expected life as a future lawyer, future husband, and future father rather quickly.

And I fully expected it. Surely, I wanted him, and I longed for the type of love affair that Adrian and Isaiah had. I was openly gay, accepted and respected, and all I needed was that ride or die manfriend who I could rely on to hold me down.

Luckily, I wasn't the longsuffering type. When I saw that Curacao was the fantasy of one night, I moved on. JJ would always be my friend, but I'd be a goddamned fool to waste my life pining away for him.

That was Sylvia's job.

I'm not a hater. I swear, I'm not. I respect other people's relationships. But Sylvia Gibbs was just a bitch.

She wasn't a bitch because she had the man that I wanted.

Well, she was a bitch for that, too.

She was a bitch because she was one of these churchy black girls who went off to college and imposed her values on everybody else. Heaven forbid a black girl wants to wear booty shorts on a hot spring day. She and her religious black girl brigade would brand her with a scarlet letter.

I noticed shit like that. I saw when women treated other women poorly for being their authentic selves. Those women—the victims of such judgment—were usually my staunchest allies and closest friends.

But it wasn't merely her judgment of other women. It was that she seemed to be rewarded for her bad personality. She was constantly on the Dean's List at Simmons. She had gotten into the city-wide chapter of the sorority of her choice on the first try. She always received scholarships and awards and internships and everything she possibly fucking wanted.

Oh my God. I couldn't *stand* her.

JJ was nothing like her beneath the surface. JJ wanted people to think he was this gruff, intense, super-hazing overachiever. He was truly a sensitive sweetheart. I'd say that even if I wasn't attracted to him.

I wasn't certain what he saw in her other than the end game: this was a woman who, if he stayed with her, would be the perfect wife and mother. She'd never go to the club and get into a fight. She'd never cheat or stray. She had high earning potential—I guess straight dudes liked all that shit, right?

And *yeah yeah*, she was pretty fucking beautiful. She was tall— almost as tall as me, and a few inches on JJ. She was as dark as midnight, slender, and lovely. She had tits and ass—more than a handful—and a slim waist. Her hair, nails, and makeup were always done to perfection and her clothes, whether name brand or not, always looked tailor-made for her.

We had met a few times and she was formal toward me, even icy. I was certain she had issues with gay people that she would never verbalize to JJ, lest he give her a tongue lashing for being intolerant toward his favorite fraternity brothers.

Oh well. Fuck her.

Over the next few months after JJ and I came to DC, he settled into the law school routine and I settled into nine-to-five life at my consulting firm. To be honest, I had no idea what I was doing there. I had double-majored in Econ and African American studies when I was at Harvard and I had gone to all the career fairs like everyone else. Consulting looked interesting and more lucrative than teaching, or continuing to grad school right away, so I played the game and landed a job in the consulting division at Concord.

What did I do? I was part of a team that got paid to tell businesses how fucked up they were. Then we'd tell them how to fix whatever it was that needed fixing. I focused specifically on fixing the community engagement and outreach arms of organizations. Basically, if it was an airline, I'd tell them how to give away vouchers to nonprofits. If it was a hotel, I'd tell them how to choose high school conferences for partnerships.

The work wasn't hard and having the Harvard name took me far. I was happy, but something nagged at me the whole time.

Members of my fraternity always drilled in me that one degree was not enough, even if it was a Harvard degree. Yet, I didn't love anything enough to go back to school for it, except photography.

I talked about this dilemma from time to time with one of my work homegirls, Kate, a friendly white woman around my age with a short, jet black bob. A Swarthmore alumna, she faced the same challenges: work or go back to school. She and I had even gone so far as to print out the brochure for a photography program at University of New Mexico that I'd heard good things about. I printed it out and read it, but never took further action.

New Mexico was *far*. And DC made me happy, for now.

On this summer afternoon, I sat in my windowless office working on a report evaluating minority outreach for a medium-sized hotel chain. I listened to old school R&B, mouthing the words while I worked. My small office would have been a drab gray if I had not decorated the walls and cabinets with my photography. All day long, I was surrounded by the people and things that I'd loved over the past few years, from the Curacao sunset to a Beta probate show. My parents were on the wall, as was my sister. And though I'd been in DC for two years, I'd quickly fallen in love with the darker side of the city—those things you didn't see if the National Mall was your sole point of reference. I had photos of Malcolm X Park (I learned quickly to never call it Meridian Hill Park to a true Washingtonian), the Arboretum, U Street, and Anacostia.

A soft knock on the door interrupted the quiet of my office. I swiveled around in my chair and leaned over to open the door. On the other side was my coworker Kate.

"Hey Kate! What's up?" I asked.

"Tony wants to see the team in the conference room."

"Right now? No email?"

"He just sent me to come get you."

"Well shit, let's go."

I followed Kate's intense walk toward the conference room, hoping it wasn't bad news that summoned us there.

Kate opened the conference room door and hurried in. Once I saw that the room was dark, I already knew what it was.

"Surprise!"

"Happy birthday!"

My team had assembled to wish me an early happy birthday. I beamed.

After they sang to me and I blew out the sole candle, the lights came up.

"Thanks guys! I really appreciate this. Wow."

"Eustace, we just wanted to get together and show you some appreciation," my boss Tony said. "You know I'll never forget your birthday because it's always around the same time you came to work with us. You've done such a bang-up job here and you're just as kind and personable as you are professional. I hope you're with us for a long time to come."

"Thank you so much Tony, wow. Thank you."

"Enjoy some cake!" he said with a smile. Kate had already cut slices for us and passed out plates. About a dozen team members filled the room and I knew them all well. Traveled with them to site visits and conferences. Hung out with them at happy hours after work. Attended house warmings and baby showers. They were a good group. I wish I could remember their names.

We chit-chatted for about twenty minutes before Tony took me to the side. He was a tall, middle-aged white guy who had lost his hair gracefully. No comb-overs for this guy.

"I had wanted to schedule this with you sooner, but things have been so crazy, especially with that conference we just ended. Listen. Today's payday. Your check is finally going to be reflective of what I think you're worth. I'm really glad to have you here and I want to keep you here for as long as I can."

"Man, thank you Tony. I appreciate that."

"And I appreciate you. Your official promotion letter is in your inbox now. Enjoy your birthday."

"I certainly will, Tony."

After Tony left, we mingled and chatted for a few more minutes. The team slowly trickled out until Kate and I remained.

"So...you got the raise, right?" Kate asked.

I nodded excitedly.

"Good. It's about time."

"Yeah. I need more money for alcohol."

Kate guffawed.

"I know you're going to live it up this weekend," she said.

"I guess so. I don't have any major plans."

"That's a damn lie," she said. I laughed.

"Well maybe I'm hanging out with the fellas tonight. But I swear I have no other plans."

"Whatever! You're turning what, 24 years old? I can guarantee you that you will be out all night at the hottest nightclub, sleep until tomorrow evening, hit up a lounge on U Street, and go to brunch on Sunday. And somehow, by the grace of almighty God, you will be sober enough to be the first one at work on Monday morning—like you always are."

"Who told you to know me so well?" I teased.

"You're pretty amazing, Eustace. Never met anybody quite like you. And I hope you really do have a happy birthday."

She stood and stretched her arms for a hug and I accepted. She was a cool girl. Maybe we'd get closer someday if I ever lifted my embargo on making work friends into "real" friends.

"And Eustace?"

"Yeah?"

"Apply to the program. See what happens."

"Maybe I will, Kate. We'll see." She smiled and walked away.

My coworkers clocked out when they saw that Tony had been the first one out the building. Any work we left behind would be there come Monday morning. It was now time to enjoy that chunk of time devoted to ourselves.

I lived in a not-so-deluxe apartment not-quite-in-the-sky on the recently gentrified intersection at 13th and U Streets. The rent was hella expensive, but for the convenience, it was worth it. I could walk downstairs to a Thai restaurant, sushi bar, and a Mexican restaurant all on the same corner. Across the street was a pharmacy and convenience store, and a Starbucks was near that. The subway, which the locals called the Metro, also had a stop right there. If I ran fast enough on a rainy day, I wouldn't even need an umbrella.

My third-floor apartment had a great view of the action on the corner. Although I was rarely home, on those occasions that I needed to recharge or work remotely, I could sit at a stool in my kitchen and watch folks pass by while I sipped my coffee.

I had a one-bedroom apartment, but it was spacious—

considering I didn't come in with a lot of stuff. I had purchased the barest of essentials once I moved in: a bedroom set, a living room set, and a television. Home was just a place to eat and sleep as far as I was concerned. I wasn't big on entertaining. Being at home for long periods made me go crazy with boredom.

Tonight was the "white party" at Renard's, a huge club across the street from the Washington Convention Center. Adrian had turned me on to this four-story mega club a few years back when the fraternity would have national board meetings in town. He had some sort of connection to the owners, so it was no great inconvenience for the bouncers to let us on up to the upper floors, especially since they knew that I wouldn't cause trouble.

It was at Renard's that Adrian started calling me "baby bro." When he introduced me to the owner, he casually said "and this is baby bro, Eustace." Renard looked me up and down, greeted me as simply "baby bro" and told me if I was good with Adrian, I was good with him.

I stood in my bedroom with the ironing board out and the overhead lights blazing. In contrast to my spartan living room, my bedroom walls were adorned with framed enlargements of my favorite photographs from over the years, some of which were the same images I had at the office. In one corner I had framed photos of all my favorite fraternal images: the old Bros strolling at Adrian's wedding, my neos' probate show from undergrad, my first national convention. Interspersed among the photos were my paddle collection, including ones I bought for myself and those that were made for me by friends and brothers.

I wasn't sure if I liked the outfit I had chosen to wear for the evening. White wasn't slimming on my six feet tall, wide frame. People constantly mistook me for a football player. I'd always tell them "Nah...just big."

I worked out. Not constantly, but regularly. I had always been about twenty pounds overweight growing up in St. Louis, but in college I evened out, lost the fluff, and gained muscle. Lost a little more weight when I pledged, then got into the best shape in my life by the time I graduated.

I looked at myself in the mirror and I was proud. Not vain, but happy that I had the body I wanted with hard work. My black boxer briefs held in firm, generous gifts in the front as well as the back. With a little extra work on leg day, my quads would also be where I wanted.

My cell phone, charging on my nightstand, rang as I studied myself. I hurried toward it and answered.

"Hello?" I said.

"Listen…I know you got a nice body and all, but do you really need to parade it around in front of your open window?"

"Shit, you can see me?" I ran to my window and looked down at the street. JJ was parked across the street in his gray Volvo. He leaned halfway out his car window, holding his chin with one hand, and throwing me a mischievous smile. We locked eyes and he threw the fraternity hand sign.

"Oh God," I said, hurriedly drawing the curtains.

"It was quite a show, sir," he continued.

"Did anybody else see me?" I asked while I snatched my short-sleeved linen shirt from the hanger and put it on.

"A couple of chicks were having a grand time as they walked by."

"Oh jeeze. This is embarrassing."

"Oh please. You're good."

"JJ, do you know how often I walk around this place butt ass naked without a care in the world?"

"At what times would that be?"

"Don't start. I'll be down in a minute."

"Bet."

I slid my white linen pants on and tied the drawstring tight around my waist. I slid my phone, wallet, and keys in my pocket and a stick of gum in my mouth and I was out.

I skipped the elevator and quickly went down the stairs and out the front door.

The night was muggy and the sidewalk was already crowded with summer revelers. I looked both ways and quickly darted across the street toward JJ's car. I got in and shut the door.

"Hey," I said.

"Hi," he replied.

"So…I'm ready."

"I see. You look good today, pa."

"Thank you. You not too shabby in your linen, either."

"I'll do a spin around for you when we get there."

"Cool."

Both his hands were clasping the steering wheel for dear life, but we weren't moving.

"You okay?" I asked softly.

"Me? Yeah! I'm good."

"You look a little-"

"I got you something," he interrupted.

"Oh. You did?"

"Yeah. I got it for your birthday. But then I thought you might not like it. But shit, we here, so fuck it. You want it?"

"Well goddamn. You make it sound so appealing."

He exhaled and released the steering wheel. He leaned toward me and for the briefest of moments, I thought he would kiss me. I held my breath and my eyes got wide. He reached behind me, to the back seat and dug down deep. He reemerged with a small black box.

"Here," he said, tossing the box toward me. I opened it. Inside was a dazzling gold ring in the shape of a lion's head with its mouth slightly agape. The last time we were at a Beta function, I had told him all I wanted now was a fraternity ring of some sort, and he came through with the lion ring—the highest status symbol of members of our fraternity. Tradition stated that you could only receive a lion ring as a gift—never as a purchase for yourself.

"I wanted the one with the garnet eyes but it was a little more than I could afford."

"JJ...this is awesome! I love it."

He grinned.

"But look on the inside," he said. He turned on the car's inside light so I could have a better look. I looked closely and saw the inscription in small, block letters:

E.D. L.B.L.C. Y.I.T.B. J.J.C.

"Eustace Dailey... Let Brotherly Love Continue... Yours in the Bond... Jeremy Jacob Carter," he said softly.

"It's perfect." I put it on one finger after the other, trying to figure out which one fit the best.

"Here, give it to me," he said. I handed him the ring and he took my right hand into his.

"It's supposed to go on the ring finger on the right hand," he said softly as he slipped it on. "There. Perfect."

He held onto my hand and stared intently at the ring.

"Thank you, JJ. I really like it." He nodded and continued holding my hand.

"We should get to Renard's. The Bros are probably all there by now." He nodded.

"Let's go," he said. He revved the engine and we were off.

Renard's, of course, was jumping. Hours after we had arrived, the club was packed with people, mostly young black professionals under the age of 30. In addition to the white linen party, there was to be a special guest performer, this emerging hip-hop and rock fusion performer named Julian. He hadn't even arrived as of 1am, but the liquor flowed endlessly so we didn't mind as we mingled up on the fourth-floor mezzanine.

Brothers and friends surrounded me on all sides, plying me with all types of cocktails. I didn't care what the ingredients were—I was just along for the ride.

As I chatted with Nina Bradley and my brother Micah Warner, I got a tap on my shoulder. Nina's eyes widened slightly and then narrowed to slits as she adjusted her posture and pushed her tits out ever so slightly.

I turned around and saw one of my new buddies, Miles Johnson. He was a tall, slim kid with broad shoulders, a narrow waist, and big feet. His long dreadlocks were cornrowed straight back.

"Hey man!" I stood up, pretending not to be slightly dizzy, and gave him a big hug.

"Happy birthday Eustace!" he said.

"Thanks man! I'm glad you made it out!"

"Wouldn't miss it. I got you something."

He handed me a gold gift bag with red paper.

"Oh shit, thank you." I took the bag and sat.

"Are you going to introduce us to your handsome friend?" Nina asked.

Micah glared at her.

"What? He *is* handsome!"

Micah rolled his eyes and stood up.

"I'm Micah."

"My name is Miles Johnson. Pleased to meet you."

"You frat?" he asked.

"No sir, I'm not."

"He's gonna be on the fall line, probably," I said flippantly while going through the bag. Miles' eyes got huge while Nina laughed.

"I'm Nina," she said, stretching her hand to Miles. "Don't mind Eustace. He's not usually this indiscreet. It's the alcohol."

Miles smiled.

"I don't mind. He's a good dude."

"Dude!" I exclaimed with his gifts in my hands.

"What the fuck you got, man?" Micah asked.

"He got me *Annie Leibovitz: American Music* and a portable hard drive. A portable hard drive my nigga?! And Annie Leibovitz? I fucking love that bitch!"

Nina and Micah laughed. I rose and gave Miles a bear hug, lifting him momentarily.

"You deserve it man. Happy birthday," he said calmly.

I sat back down and looked at Nina and Micah with my smiling mouth agape.

"So, how do you know each other?" Nina asked us.

"We've worked on some photography projects together," Miles said.

"Oh, you're a photographer as well?" Micah asked.

"Naw, I be shooting him, though," I said.

"Oh," Nina said.

"You're a model?" Micah asked.

"Actually I'm starting library school next month," Miles said.

"Library school?" Nina asked.

"Who's going to library school?" JJ said as he arrived with two drinks.

"What's this?" I asked.

"A fireball? Some shit," he said.

"I ain't even finish the last drink." I said.

"Double fist it, nigga," he said. I sadly shook my head and accepted his drink.

"So who's going to library school?" JJ asked again.

"I am," Miles said.

"And who the fuck are you?" JJ asked.

"My name is Miles Johnson," he said.

"Oh, you're Miles Johnson," JJ repeated. "You went to Georgetown, right?"

"Yes, sir."

"And aren't you going to Maryland in the fall?"

"Yes, sir. I'll be getting a Master's degree in Library Science," he said.

"So like...you really do want to be a librarian, huh?" Micah said.

"Yes, sir. I fell in love with books and libraries when I was a kid watching *Reading Rainbow*. I knew early on that I wanted to have all the power in the universe, so I had to be a librarian."

JJ spit out a little of his drink and Nina stifled a laugh.

"All the power in the universe, though?" Micah asked.

"Yes, sir! Have you ever heard that books can take you to a new world? Well I believe that. Books can teach you anything you need to know. Books can make you smarter and more talented. They can heal...and they can save. And I wanted to read all the books and introduce others to reading. I knew I would be a librarian. And now I'm on my way."

Awkward silence.

"Isn't that awesome guys?" I asked excitedly.

"So apparently you want to be a Beta?" JJ asked.

"Yes, I do," Miles replied.

"Why didn't you pledge at Georgetown?" JJ asked pointedly.

"As you probably know, there is no Greek life at Georgetown-"

"There's none at Potomac, either," Micah interrupted. "Which is right next door to Georgetown. Why didn't you try to join Sigma Chapter?"

"Georgetown is not on the charter of Sigma Chapter, so even though I had attended Sigma Chapter's events, I would have needed special permission to-"

"Did you attend rush?" JJ asked.

"I made the decision to focus on my studies rather than pursue membership as an undergraduate. I wanted to pursue it, but I wanted to finish strong and get funding for graduate school." Miles explained.

"So what was your GPA?" Micah asked.

"4.0."

"Excuse me?" JJ asked.

"I graduated with a 4.0 grade point average," Miles clarified.

"In your last semester, right?" JJ asked.

"Cumulative."

"Well…I'll be damned!" JJ laughed.

"Told you. The boy is a bad motherfucker." I elbowed JJ in the ribs. He laughed more.

"Eustace told me all about you, but he ain't tell me that," JJ said.

"But let's talk about the modeling," Nina said.

"Here we go," Micah groaned.

"You hush. You know I am the officially unofficial supreme basileus of the Beta Babes, Incorporated, and I need to vet the candidate. Now baby…Miles… do Eustace have you posing butterball naked? You know that's hazing and you don't have to submit to it?"

"I can assure you that me and Eustace's relationship is on the up-and-up," Miles said.

"Okay. Cuz I don't wanna have to report him. He's an old nasty buzzard, if you didn't know. Just like Adrian." she quipped.

"Mannnn I ain't never touched Miles," I said.

"Not yet! I know you, boy. Miles come in with these broad shoulders and all this hair, and I was like-"

"Anyway," Micah interrupted. "I'm looking forward to getting to know you better. Good luck."

"Thank you, sir."

"And you know I was just messing with you, boo. Eustace is one of the better Betas I've met over the years."

"But nobody will ever replace your precious Adrian Collins," JJ said.

"Well of course not. Nobody's perfect." She winked.

Our busy VIP area became three people deeper within moments. Two big, bodyguard types entered, followed by a tall, lean light-skinned dude with platinum blond hair. His skin, exposed by his tight sleeveless t-shirt, was tatted from his wrists to his shoulders. He had silver bracelets on each wrist, rings on multiple fingers, and diamond stud earrings in both ears. He had on skinny white jeans and what appeared to be silver and white Jordans.

"He's festive," I said.

"How y'all doing?" he asked.

"We good. It's my birthday," I said.

"Oh, is it?" he asked. I nodded.

"Who are you though?" I asked.

"You'll see," he said. One of his security folks handed him a microphone.

This nigga just walks around with a microphone though? I asked myself.

"Aye, what's your name man?" he asked.

"Eustace." I said.

"Eustace? Like the little homie from *Voyage of the Dawn Treader*?"

I nodded excitedly that he was familiar with who I had been named after.

"Well Eustace," he began, turning on the microphone. "My name is Julian. And I just wanna say…happy birthday…happy birthday, man."

"Is he singing to me?!" I asked Nina.

"Chile!"

"I said…I just wanna say… happy birthday… happy birthday… happy birthday."

As his voice filled both the room and the club's sound system, we heard the downstairs dance floor erupt with screams.

Julian shook my hand and walked over to the railing separating us from the partygoers below.

"I said it's my boy Eustace's birthday!" he shouted to the crowd below. Pandemonium ensued. The stage where he was supposed to perform was empty and the crowd shifted to below our perch.

"Come on up here, Eustace!" he called back to me. I got out of my chair and focused on walking toward him without falling.

"How old are you today, Eustace?" he asked, putting the mic in my face.

"24," I said. The crowd below cheered. He put his arm around my shoulder.

"Y'all, I want you to sing happy birthday to my boy Eustace before I begin my set, aight? One, two, three!"

The entire club below us serenaded me and I smiled the whole time. Nobody had ever done anything like this for me before. As the song concluded, I waved to the crowd and they cheered again.

"Enjoy your birthday man," he said, shaking my hand and drawing me into a hug. Camera flashes went off around us.

"But just so y'all know? MY NAME IS JULIAN!"

I stepped back as Julian's backing track filled the club and the audience began to bounce.

"So that's Julian! I know this song," I told Nina.

"I got some pictures on my camera!" she said.

"Good! I didn't feel like bringing my big ass camera with me."

"Here, take this. Take pictures of him!"

"Oh my God I can't. I'm way too drunk."

"You got this! Take the damn camera."

Nina had a digital point and shoot camera with a pretty good optical zoom on it. I looked at the label and saw that it was eight megapixels. I could work with this. I willed myself to get sober and I focused on shooting Julian's concert as though I was getting paid to do it.

He was an excellent performer. His voice was beautiful, whether he was rapping with intensity or crooning soulfully. And he was indeed sexy, playing the irreverent bad boy role to the hilt. His songs straddled the line between spiritually transcendent and absurdly crass. He was like Prince with muscles, James Brown with blond curls, and Eazy-E with a softer touch, all wrapped into one.

From start to finish, his entire performance was a huge mindfuck, beginning with his unorthodox performance location in the venue. I mean, who does that? Who comes to the club and is like "Nah, I don't want to perform on stage, I'm gonna perform on this mezzanine?" Julian did, that's who. The entire time, people preened their necks to see what he would do next.

His lyrical content was ambiguous at best—women loved him, but it wasn't clear if he sang to them or their dates. Even though his outfit and look were questionable, he rapped tough, as though he had flown in from the hardest block in South Central Los Angeles.

I liked this guy.

I took a lot of crowd shots and I quickly saw that I was late to the Julian party. Those men and women knew exactly who he was and they sang along with all his songs, word for word. He thrived on that energy and each song he performed was even more intense than the last.

By the end of the third song, his entire t-shirt was drenched in sweat. He took it off and threw it into the crowd, where it was ripped into two by a guy and a girl who desperately needed it. If Julian hadn't been all about love and sex as part of his routine, a riot could have broken out. But not with his fans.

I got a lot of close-ups of Julian while he performed. Sweat streamed down his forehead and settled into pools above his collarbone before they overflowed and fell down his chest. He was a walking contradiction, somehow both skinny and muscular, something like a dancer. He had an ass that sat high and ample, though. I wasn't sure if he was my type, but if I saw him walking down the street by himself, I'd look more than once in his direction.

When he saw me taking pictures, he smiled wide and rapped a few bars in my direction. He was animated, playing directly into the lens as though I was recording video. Luckily, I knew how to adjust the settings on Nina's simple camera to optimize the low-powered flash.

After about six songs, he was done. While the crowd cheered he shook my hand one more time and pulled me to him. I put my hand on the sweaty small of his back for balance.

"Come with me," he whispered. He grabbed my hand and led me away from the crowd. One of his massive security guards led us down a dark hallway. Julian didn't drop my hand once. I took one glance back and saw his second security guard towering behind me.

We walked down a long, narrow hallway and the DJ's music faded away. We brushed against the club's various servers and hostesses who paused and eyed Julian from his face to his hand, still connected with mine.

We made a sharp turn left into a small dressing room with a single chair and vanity. His security left us alone in the room and quietly closed the door behind them.

He finally faced me and smiled.

"What did you think?" he asked.

"You were...amazing." I couldn't contain my smile. He returned it.

"Thank you. I'm glad to make your birthday more special." He sat down at the vanity and produced a bottle of water from a cooler underneath.

"You don't even know me," I said.

"Sure I do. Eustace Scrubb. Chronicles of Narnia. Born 24 years ago today." He winked.

"It's Dailey. Eustace Dailey." I smiled.

"Even better," he said. He guzzled half a bottle of water. I watched his Adam's apple bob with each gulp.

"You officially know more about me than I know about you." I leaned against the wall with my hands in my pockets.

"You heard my music before?"

"Some."

"If you've ever heard my music, then you already know me."

"Maybe I want to know more."

"Julian Bennett. From Miami."

"Oh, for real? That explains that tan."

"Damn right."

"I mean, you still light as hell, but you got that golden brown to you."

"I'm not that damn light," he scoffed. I laughed.

"So you one of them light-skinned deniers. I gotcha."

"Anyway...born and raised in Miami. Went to FAMU. Drum Major for the Marching 100. Graduated. Moved to Atlanta to try to start my music career. Made a few mixtapes and a few independent albums. Made some damn good music that nobody bought. Came back down to Miami. Waited tables for a while. Worked the shit out of the internet and finally got noticed by a decent manager who invested in my career the way a manager should. Now I'm finally here, living my dream at age 30."

"You 30?"

"Damn right!"

"You don't look it."

"I don't know what 30 is supposed to look like. I just focus on being myself."

I smiled and nodded.

"You really spent your 20s taking care of business, huh?"

"Got to. The music don't make itself and it don't sell itself. I wasn't born into a musical dynasty—my family was supportive, but they ain't know what to tell me to do. And college was fun, but while I was in class, a lot more people who were a lot less talented were beginning their careers. My degree meant nothing when it came to building an empire."

"You regret going to school?"

"I wouldn't trade FAMU for anything. I'm just glad I am where I am now."

"That's dope," I said.

"What about you? What are you all about?"

"Shit. Consulting for Concord. And taking pictures."

"So you a real photographer, huh?"

"Something like that." Heavy knocks at the door punctuated my sentence.

"Yo?" Julian called.

"The car service is downstairs," the guard said through the door.

"Bet!" Julian stood.

"I guess this is goodbye," I said extending my hand to him. He shook my hand and pulled me toward him, hugging me tightly.

"It doesn't have to be," he said. His hands rubbed my back in small circles. I closed my eyes and rested my head on his shoulder. He smelled faintly of cologne. The stubble on our cheeks rubbed together as I finally lifted my head

"Maybe another time." I stood face to face with him, with my hands on his sides.

"Another time then, Eustace Dailey." He smiled and gently rubbed my shoulders.

Julian produced a sheer white hoodie from behind the door and placed a set of rhinestone sunglasses on his face, looking every bit the rock star he wanted to be. We hurried through the hallway and returned to the VIP area where I'd left my friends. We stopped, and he grabbed me by the waist again.

"Send me those pictures, aight?" he said in my ear.

"Where you want me to send them?" I asked.

"My website. I check all my own email. I'll get it."

"No doubt."

"Thanks, sexy. See you later." He kissed me on the cheek and hurried off with his security detail. I walked back to my chair.

"What...the fuck...was that?" Micah asked. His brown face, usually the pinnacle of collectedness, was awash with amazement. Nina and JJ sat in silent wonderment.

"Dude...I don't even know," I said.

"Always an adventure with Eustace Dailey," JJ said with an ever-so-slight roll of his eyes.

His jealously was endearing. He passed me a bottle of water, which I happily accepted with a smile.

"I'm surprised you ain't going back to Julian's hotel room," JJ said with a slight attitude. I had said my farewells to my friends and brothers, and JJ and I were back in his car, on the way to my place once again.

"Who said I'm not?" I snapped back.

"Touchy," he said.

"Don't start, JJ. You always get like this when somebody takes an interest in me."

"You saying I'm jealous?"

"Aren't you?"

"Man…you buggin'."

The mood in the car soured and the air was thick with tension between us.

"What did you think of Miles?" I asked, hoping to lighten the mood.

"He's a fucking weirdo."

"He marches to the beat of his own drum."

"Yeah, that's what I said: a fucking weirdo. How did you meet him?"

"On a website for photographers and models."

"Oh really? You sure you weren't trolling for a date?"

"You know what, JJ? Pull over."

"Why? We're almost at your spot."

"Pull over right now. We need to talk."

JJ parked the car next to a small dog park. We were in those last moments of darkness where everything slept, or at least remained still.

"What the fuck are we really doing, JJ?"

"I don't know."

"Why are you treating me like this?"

"I don't know, Eustace. I'm just…everything's upside-down."

"Why?"

JJ was silent.

"JJ, what's wrong. Tell me."

"I wanted to tell you first, before it happens."

"What?"

"I'm going to propose to Sylvia," JJ said finally.

"What?! Are you fucking kidding me?"

"I'm going to do it sometime before the end of the summer."

I sighed.

"I want you to be okay with this."

"What are you, crazy or just stupid?"

"Why are you so fucking mean?"

"Sylvia is a bitch. Why would you propose to her?" I whined.

"Please don't call my girlfriend a bitch."

"Okay, Sylvia's not a bitch. But she's definitely excelling in the art of bitchiness."

JJ cackled.

"See, you know I ain't lying."

"She has her moments. But it's what you don't see, Eustace. Listen. I've known her for years now, and yeah, she can be a lot to handle. But I handle her. She's pushed me to be better since day one. She's smart, she's sexy, she's talented. And she's spiritual. I love that about her. I love her."

"And she's the one you want to spend your life with."

"She's the woman I want to start a family with."

"Interesting choice of words."

"You *know* I'm precise. Listen man...in another year, I'm going to be a lawyer. She's going to have a divinity degree in a few more years. She's held me down, now I have to hold her down. I like her, man. I like her a lot. She makes me better."

"Okay."

"I hope that you'll support me on this."

"JJ? Really? What the fuck? How is it that you can get all pissy when it seems a guy wants to be with me, but you demand my support when it comes to you and Sylvia?"

"I can't help it. Yes, I get fucking jealous when there's another guy in your life. Of course I am. You want to know why? Because I know they're ready. They're confident. They're brave. They're a match for you. They give you a whole lot of things that a guy like me can't give you. And that fucks me up."

"But above all else, we're still friends. And friends should want friends to be happy."

"Yes. I agree with you. Friends want the best for each other. So what's the problem with me marrying Sylvia? Really, what does it change between us?"

"The problem is...shit..."

"What?" JJ asked.

"The problem is I just want you to be happy. That's all. Everything else is for me to work out."

"I want you to be happy, too. I mean that."

"If I explore this thing with Miles…if there is a thing…will you be okay with that?"

"Do you think there will be a thing?"

"I don't know. Maybe."

"I promise you I won't have a problem if it becomes a thing."

"You really mean it?"

"I really do. Can you be happy for me when I propose to Sylvia?"

"I can try. Hard."

"Okay. That's all I can ask."

"Okay."

We sat in silence for a long time. The sun started to rise and I didn't even feel drunk anymore.

"I should take you home now," he said.

"Okay."

He started the car and sped down the street. We arrived in moments.

"I'll walk you to the door," he said.

"Don't."

"No?"

"No. I'll be fine."

"Okay, well,"

"JJ. If this is going to be it, then this needs to be it."

"I understand."

"We can't go back and forth."

"I agree."

"It's just that…how we feel…"

"Yeah…it's going to be hard. You know. Letting go. For real."

"Yeah."

We sat in silence for a few more moments.

"You know…I've never felt this intensely for someone I've never had sex with," I said.

"We've never even kissed. Not for real."

"Have you ever kissed a man?"

"Hell no!"

"Well you don't have to say it like that."

"I'm sorry. I didn't mean it how it sounded. There's never been another dude. Ever. Only you."

"You think you could go your entire life without kissing a dude?"

"No."

"No?"

"Not if that means I've never kissed you."

"JJ. Dammit."

"I know."

"I mean, you do kind of owe me, though."

"Owe you? How you figure?"

"All the shit you put me through? Yeah, you probably owe me a lot more than that."

"Me! You wildin' nigga! You put me through just as-"

I kissed him.

To shut him up, I kissed him.

To seal the deal we had made to respect each other's boundaries, I kissed him. Hard, deep, infinitely—we kissed.

Years of frustration, anger, sadness, hurt, all the negative emotions that came with falling in love with my best friend—I wanted those things to disappear. If I could just taste him once, I could let everything else fall away. I could focus on the rest of my life. I could move on. I could support him how he needed to be supported, even if he was going to marry that bitch. And he could support me in a meaningful relationship with a man, the first he'd ever see me in.

This thing between us had to end, but I needed to know what his lips felt like on mine. His mouth opened easily and my tongue slid through. I touched his face with my hand and gently pushed him away.

"No matter what happens…I will always love you," I said.

He nodded and stared at me with the saddest, most hopeful eyes.

"Text me when you get home," I instructed. He nodded once again.

I left the car and entered my apartment building. I had the sensation of an out-of-body experience, and whether that was the beginnings of my hangover or the aftereffects of my first kiss with JJ was unknown to me. I floated, floated, up the elevator, through the door, and into my bed, where I wept silently until I fell asleep.

I woke in the middle of the afternoon on Saturday and decided that I would apply to the MFA program in photography at University of

New Mexico after all. I clicked "send" on the electronic application, paid the application fee, and gave it no further thought.

Late Sunday morning, I was finally awake enough to answer my phone.

"Happy birthday, friend!" Miles said cheerfully on the other end.

"Thank you, man."

"Damn you sound like shit," he deadpanned.

"I feel better than I sound, I think."

"I just got out of church. Let me take you to brunch. There's this spot in Adams Morgan that does unlimited mimosas."

"Oh my God. I think I might drop dead if I have one more drink."

"Okay, okay. No mimosas for you. But you'll still let me treat you, right?"

"Yes, yes of course. What time?"

"Can you be ready in twenty minutes?"

"I sure can. See you soon."

I hung up, yawned, and stretched my body. Time to make it happen.

I took a quick shower and threw on a screen-printed fraternity t-shirt and khaki shorts. I was sure to lotion my body up—my mom had drilled it into me from an early age that nobody wanted to see my ashy limbs or crusty feet. When I was sufficiently greased up, I put my flip-flops on and headed downstairs.

Miles was already there, as I knew he would be. He was notoriously early.

He drove a whimsical, lime green VW Beetle. I got into the passenger seat and shook his hand.

"When you gonna get another car, man?"

"I have a car, Eustace."

"Yeah, but doesn't it make you feel bad that little kids all across this city punch each other every time they see you drive down the street?"

"I get a kick out of it, actually."

I laughed. Miles did have a sense of humor, but not like the rest of the guys I hung out with. My people were loud, gregarious, and raunchy. Miles was mild-mannered and had a dry wit. While my boys watched reruns of *Martin*, Miles was more likely to be found watching *Monty Python's Flying Circus*.

He was a handsome dude. His dreadlocks were cornrowed tightly toward the back of his head and secured with small black bands at the end. His profile was stunning—which was a big reason that I enjoyed photographing him. He had both soft and hard features at the same time. His large nose pointed slightly downward and his eyebrows were naturally arched high, giving him somewhat of a sinister look if you didn't know him, but his cheeks, forehead, chin, and eyes were all soft and round. His large brown hands casually held the steering wheel.

"What are you thinking about?" he asked.

"Nothing. Just looking at your face. Thinking about our next project."

"I was thinking some black and white portraits would be nice. I was looking through some photos from the old WPA freed slave photographs and I thought they were striking."

"What's 'WPA?'"

"The United States Works Progress Administration. In the early 1900s they went around interviewing former slaves to document their stories. They also took a bunch of pictures, too."

"That sounds really cool."

"It is. When I get my own library, I'm gonna do an exhibit on that. Not during black history month, though. People need to know these things year-round."

"I totally agree with that, man."

"Right. But you know what's crazy? I looked through those pictures and I swear I've seen a dude around DC who looks just like a guy in those photos. I mean exactly like him, man! Out of these dozens of elderly folks was this one old man who didn't look that old at all. I mean he was sitting down with a hat on, but that face hardly had a wrinkle."

"That's crazy."

"Yeah. Must be his ancestor or something."

"Probably so. We all have a double somewhere. Hey, did you have fun Friday night?"

"Did I! Man, Julian?! Julian came to your party!"

"Well I wouldn't put it like that. More like we partied at Julian's concert."

"But he put you up there man! That was dope. And he kissed you on the cheek! Did you wash your face yet?"

I laughed heartily.

"Yes, I washed my face. Truth be told, I had no idea who Julian was before that night. Like, I'd heard of him, but I didn't know how big he was."

"Oh man, when his mixtape dropped a few months ago, all the Georgetown folks were going crazy over it. I guess the whole album is dropping this fall."

"I'm looking forward to it now that I know who he is. Hey, that's the spot, right?" I gestured toward the restaurant on Columbia Road.

"Yup, and there's a parking space right there," Miles said. He slid his little green monster into that space with the precision of a surgeon.

"Good job," I said, impressed.

"Thank you."

We emerged from the car and walked to the restaurant, which was not terribly crowded. Miles asked for a table for two and we were led to a distant corner.

"Hey, I have a question for you," I asked Miles.

"Shoot."

"Micah and JJ...they didn't make you uncomfortable with their questions, did they?"

"Oh, no. Not at all."

"Good. You know it only gets worse from here on in."

"Oh."

"You will be tested every step of the way by a lot of people. Beta Chi Phi is a small organization. Nobody sneaks in. Everyone is vetted. Trust me when I tell you if there is anything you haven't disclosed that would be embarrassing to you, it will be discovered. You hear me?"

"Yes, I do. I have definitely told you all there is to know about me."

"The fact that you are fresh out of undergrad and you didn't even try to pledge an undergrad chapter, or start your own—that will continue to be a problem for you. I hope you're ready for the onslaught."

"I am. All I can do is tell my truth and hope the members like me anyway."

I nodded slowly and sipped my mimosa, from which I had previously pledged to abstain.

"I've been wanting to ask you something, too," Miles said.

"What is it?"

"I know that joining a graduate chapter of a fraternity is going to be different from pledging an undergraduate chapter. I don't expect to do a lot of the same things, you know? But I don't want to be...how can I put this politely? I really don't want to be known as 'paper.' *If* I'm selected for membership, that is. I want to have as full an experience as possible."

"Oh, you want to be made?"

"Yes. Yes, I do."

"That's good to know."

"Do you think that's a possibility?"

"Anything's possible."

"I see."

"So, when are you trying to do another shoot?" I shifted gears.

"I'm down any weekend you're free."

"Let's try to get one more in before you start grad school. I'm sure you'll be pretty busy come the end of August."

"Yeah, I will be."

Silently, I went through my head to figure out who was in "the circle." Me, Micah, and JJ for sure, representing Beta, Sigma, and Alpha chapters. Couldn't too much fool with the Bros at UDC or Howard—they were an entirely different breed all together. The Bros from Maryland would also need to be in the loop as well, since Miles would be on their campus every day.

Yeah, Miles would be having a "real" pledge process. Sooner than he thought.

"I need you to call JJ and Micah."

"Right now?" Miles asked.

"No, not right now. But this evening. And every evening at seventy minutes past seven until they tell you otherwise."

"Okay," he said. He hadn't even missed a beat. This boy was ready to be pledged.

"How about you?" he asked.

"Me?"

"When do you want your phone call?"

"Make sure I'm up every morning at seventy past seven. I got to be at work on time."

"Okay," he said.

"What's the significance of that time?" I asked.

"Seventy past seven... because Beta Chi Phi was founded in 1970. Nineteen hundred hours... seventy minutes... 8:10pm. And seven hundred hours plus seventy minutes is 8:10am."

"Good. Stay on your toes," I said.

"I will. And...thank you."

I nodded and restrained my grin. Good God, I loved pledging season.

Dear Julian,

I hope this message finds you well. I'm Eustace Dailey. We met at your DC performance last week. I just wanted to say thank you for helping to make my birthday special. It was one for the history books. I really enjoyed your performance and I like your music in general—I think you'll go far.

I hope you enjoy the photos I've linked. It was just a little point-and-shoot camera, but I think you'll like the final product.

I do a little photography myself, and if I'd had my own camera, the pictures would have been even better.

Anyway, let me know if you like them when you get a chance. I'd love feedback.

Regards,
Eustace Dailey

Dear Eustace Dailey,

Wow. My man. These photos are super dope. May I have your permission to post them on my website? I'd give you the proper credit.

Thanks for letting me incorporate your birthday into my performance. You and your friends looked like you were already having an awesome time. I'm glad I got to be a small part of it.

One love,
Julian

Dear Julian,

Of course you can post the pictures. No credit necessary. Please stay in touch. I'd love to link up the next time you're in DC.

Regards,
Eustace

Dear Eustace Dailey,

I always give proper credit.

And I will definitely let you know the next time I'm in DC.

One love,
Julian

Chapter Two:
Early August 2005

After I got back from Curacao in 2003, I decided to take my photography more seriously. My photos from Adrian and Isaiah's wedding were damn good, and I was especially pleased after I saw the enlargements. I sent the newlyweds a box of prints shortly after the wedding, and a framed, poster-sized print for a Christmas gift. They were ecstatic.

I didn't take any classes, but I read books and websites about the craft while on breaks from work. I bought new items like a tripod, my first set of lights, and a paper backdrop kit. Later came the strobe, a vinyl backdrop, and a light meter.

The most important thing I did for myself as a photographer was to stay in the habit of taking pictures. It was a rare occasion indeed that found me without a camera. That fall of 2003, I was at all the fun shit that DC had to offer with camera in tow: the Black Family Reunion, Howard Homecoming, Halloween in Georgetown, and many neighborhood festivals. I even shot a few DC high school football games.

I created a website to share my work with the public by the time winter hit. The brotherhood was the first to see my work, and shortly thereafter, the chapters in DC were contacting me to shoot their events. By the early months of 2004, I had shot events at Potomac, Rock Creek, Howard, UDC, and most other local schools with chapters. From those events, I met a lot of sorority women who needed their events captured as well. I never accepted payment—just the occasional meal or snack if the events had any available. A few times, the brothers or the ladies would quietly give me a bottle of liquor as a thank you gift.

With spring in full bloom, I took my camera to as many probate shows as I could. I suppose I should say "new member presentations" now—the first step show that new members of black fraternities and sororities performed in as new initiates. I covered all the Beta probates, of course, and then the sororities started calling me. "Just wanted to make sure you're gonna be there!" they would say. If I said I was tired, they whined and pouted and begged until I decided to head out to their shows. Even our rival fraternities would let me know the dates of their shows well enough in advance to plan to be there. I obliged happily, though I always knew the most powerful shots would be of my own brothers.

I had a great time, every time, and every set of pictures seemed to be better than the last. My website with all the photos got larger and larger until I had to start paying extra for space and bandwidth for all the traffic I got at the site.

It was at that point that I decided I needed to start earning extra income from this hobby. I enjoyed being somewhat of a documentarian, but it would be nice if the hobby paid for itself. So that summer, the summer of 2004, I started advertising prices for various services. I thought I could book an event here or there on weekends to recoup the money I had been spending on equipment.

By the end of June, I became the photographer in residence at one of my favorite jazz clubs uptown and had booked a half-dozen baby showers and engagement parties.

It was easy work. It was fun work. And most importantly, it was paid work. I loved it.

By the time fall of 2004 rolled around, I had cut back on freebies and started to focus on figuring out what kind of photographer I wanted to be. Shooting special events was fine, but it didn't make me feel as excited as when I first started, and I wasn't capturing shots like the ones from probate shows and Adrian's wedding. I decided to start practicing portraiture and I reduced the time I spent shooting anything else.

Since I hadn't been taking time to decorate my apartment, my living room was the perfect size to double as a makeshift photography studio. One my barest wall, I installed a roller system for my various backdrops, including my favorite, which was a long roll of white vinyl. All my other stuff was collapsible and easily stored in my closets.

My first clients were my parents. When they visited me, I turned on the lights, posed them, and took a few pictures. My dad wasn't one for being photographed, but they turned out amazing.

I roped in a few of my neighbors, too, and then some coworkers. By November of 2004, I was thirsty to build my portfolio even more.

I joined a social network for models and photographers. It was sorta sketchy at first, with plenty of creepy guys with cameras preying on young women who didn't have a good handle on the fashion industry yet. But I spent time browsing the profiles, hoping I could find a muse.

I came across one profile of a guy who was simply beautiful to me. He appeared tough and gentle at the same time. He had posted a random photo of himself at some formal event. The rest of his profile was empty, save for an introduction saying he was a student in his last year at a local college and was building his portfolio because his friends kept suggesting he try modeling. So here he was.

And that guy was Miles Davis Johnson.

When I reached out to Miles, I told him honestly that I was trying to build my portfolio as well, so if he was willing to exchange his time for prints, or time for a CD of the images, then I'd gladly shoot him.

He agreed, but said he'd like to meet for coffee first to make sure I was on the up-and-up. I told him that was a great idea, since I didn't know him either.

We met at the Starbucks near my apartment and immediately hit it off. He had this way of staring at you intently while you spoke, as though his life depended on hanging on every word.

From that first coffee to three photo sessions and many chances to hang out in between, Miles and I were becoming good friends. And today would be our fourth photo shoot.

"Help me roll out this backdrop?" I asked Miles.

"Sure thing," he said. We carefully rolled out the white vinyl backdrop until it was fully extended, covering most of my hardwood living room floor.

"You got your outfits?" I asked.

"Yessir. Just some simple all-white outfits and some colorful accessories."

"Did the party inspire you?"

"Yeah. It did. I saw that you can do a lot with one color. And I knew your backdrop was white so I was curious how it would all turn out."

"No doubt! Well, you know the routine. The bathroom's right there. Take your time. I'll be ready."

"Thanks, man."

JJ and I had a raw passion between us—a complicated, painful attraction. Miles, in contrast, was an easy crush to have. When he looked at me, I felt like the only man in the world. And he trusted me, even though with every photo shoot I was more and more concerned that he'd notice my growing erection.

I've always been attracted to the flesh that I cannot see. Certainly, nudes were fun and erotic, but it was the semi-nudes which I found more titillating. Seeing a bicep peek out from an oversized shirt, or thigh meat dipping low when a man in shorts is seated, or even the small of a man's back when he is shirtless and facing away from me…those were the best parts. And Miles was all the best parts.

He emerged from the bathroom with a white tank top and tight-fitting white linen pants and no shoes. He had a chain on around his neck. Each link was a different color of the rainbow.

It was a Pride necklace; one of those ten dollar deals you buy down at the parade. No, not pride with a little p, but Pride with a big P. Gay Pride.

"Oh," I said.

"The necklace makes the whole thing pop, right?"

"Yes, it does. It's going to be a striking look."

"I think so, too."

"But Miles…this isn't what you want to do."

"Why not?" He stood with his hands on his hips.

"Miles, that's a gay pride necklace."

"Yeah, I know."

"Are you…gay?"

"Hell no! I mean, no offense. But no. I'm not gay."

I deflated on the inside. There goes our wonderful future together.

"So why the necklace?"

"I like the colors."

"Miles, if anyone sees these photos, they are probably going to think you're gay. Everybody knows what the rainbow means."

"Rainbows mean a lot of things, Eustace."

"Miles, I'm telling you. They see this, they are going to think you're gay."

"Who-"

"Everybody!"

"No, I'm not finished. Who *cares*?"

"Well shit, anybody could *care*..." I paused and pondered the question further. "...but if you don't care, I don't care. So let's take some pictures."

"Cool. And for the last set, let me direct you, okay?"

"What?"

"I had an idea for the final set we do. Just go with it, okay?"

"Well that's fine. I guess."

Miles smiled at me.

"Typical Leo. Can't relinquish any control," Miles said.

"Why anybody *wouldn't* want to be in control is beyond me," I quipped.

This boy—this man—was a damn good model. For someone so awkward and socially disconnected, he could sell a look, from head to foot, with only his eyes.

I hadn't let his admission of straightness get to me when he first said he wasn't gay, but the more I shot him, the more I posed him, the more bummed I became. It seemed like everybody I liked or connected with was straight, confused, or unavailable—or all three. Somewhere in my head, I thought maybe Miles would be the antidote for JJ. I needed a dude who was sure of himself and what he was about, and that was Miles. Nobody was going to put him in a box—ever—and nobody was going to tell him he couldn't be exactly who he wanted to be. Librarians were *cool*, dammit.

"You okay?" he asked. I nodded.

"Yeah. A little tired for some reason."

"Let's do this one last thing and we can be done, okay?"

"You the boss. What do you want to do?"

"Okay, put your camera on your tripod and sorta aim it downward. I want to get on the floor."

"Okay." Miles laid on the floor while I affixed my camera to the tripod. I loosened a big plastic screw and tilted the camera forward, looking through the viewfinder at various increments to make sure Miles was in the shot. I tightened the screw again.

"Slide up a little bit, toward the wall," I instructed. Miles scooted until his head almost touched the wall.

"How I look?" he asked.

"Good. You want me to shoot you like this?" I asked.

"No. Be patient," he said. He got off the floor and walked to my bathroom. I tinkered with my camera for a few moments.

"You know how to put that thing on a timer?" he asked me from the bathroom.

"Yeah, no problem. But why do you need that?"

"I want you to get in the picture with me."

"Nah, I'm good."

"You said you'd do it," he reminded me.

"Fine, just one." His bare feet softly slapped the floor as he walked toward the backdrop. When I finally looked up from my camera, Miles was already sitting on the floor.

Butt naked.

"Miles what the hell are you doing!" I asked.

"Taking a picture."

"We never talked about nude shots before."

"I trust you."

"It's not about trust, man. First of all, I've never shot anyone nude before. Second, what are you even going to use these for, and third, oh my God are your nuts touching my vinyl?"

Miles lifted one hip, reached between his legs, and adjusted his package.

"Sorry man, they hang low," he said.

"Oh my God. Oh my God," I looked away from Miles and began to pace the floor.

"So do you want to hear the vision?" he asked.

"Miles, I think you should put your clothes on," I said.

"Hear me out. So when I was buying your birthday present, I came across that photo that Annie Liebovitz took of John Lennon and Yoko Ono. Yoko got all her clothes on and John is naked, holding onto her for dear life. They're on the floor. You know he got killed shortly after that was taken, right?"

"Well God-willing nobody shoots you, too!"

"Man, the only thing shooting me today is gonna be your camera."

"So you want me to recreate this John and Yoko thing with you?"

"Yup!"

"Why?"

"Why not?"

"Miles…"

"Because I want to show the world that a straight dude can be completely vulnerable with a gay dude and have no worries."

"Man…really?"

"Yes, really! Eustace, you are a phenomenal photographer and I want you to take this picture. And of course, be the subject with me. I think this is gonna be a hot photo that people need to see. Not just because of the message, but because it's emblematic of our friendship. I really do trust you, like completely."

"You do?"

"Yes! You are a good dude. A talented dude. And you've been a good friend to me."

"So you repay me by stripping?"

"Man, listen to me." Miles stood up.

"Whoa, dude," I said.

"Eustace, look at me."

"I don't want to look at you naked."

"Eustace."

"Miles."

"Eustace!"

"What!"

"How many naked men have you seen in your life? Hundreds by now, right?"

"Excuse me, sir, what do you take me for?"

"A photographer! Listen, just look at me."

I raised my gaze from the floor and allowed his long and lean brown body fill my sight, from the arched soles of his feet to his strong quadriceps; from his perfect "V" muscle to his broad shoulders; from his gleaming white smile to his long dreadlocks cascading from his head to halfway down his chest.

And the dick. The dick was nice. It was thick—flaccid, but impressive in girth and length. And he was right: his balls did hang low.

"See? I'm not trying to say you've seen a bunch of naked dudes in your life. But I know you ain't no virgin. And I know you're a professional, so all this should be nothing to you, right?"

"Well, it's something."

"It's just me. See?" Miles turned 360 degrees, showing me his muscular back and ass.

"This is all of me."

"Yes, yes, I see. Miles, just tell me what you want me to do, okay? This all makes me uncomfortable."

"Relax, my man. How long is the timer on the camera?"

"I can set it for up to 30 seconds."

"Alright. Well gimme 20 seconds. Hit the button, then lay down in the middle, on your back, just like Yoko did. I'll do the rest."

I shook my head slowly.

"Okay. Just get in your place. You get one shot."

"Bet." He sat back on the floor, to the right of the center of the vinyl. I walked to the camera and found the timer setting, changing it to twenty seconds.

"You ready?" I asked.

"Yup!" he said cheerfully.

"I'm pushing the button...now."

I turned around and Miles was already patting the floor where he wanted me to lay. I got next to him and stared at the ceiling. The camera beeped once. Fifteen seconds left.

"Stiffen up a bit," he instructed. I straightened my back while he got close to me. He threw his left leg around my body, his big toe connecting to the ground on my right side. The camera beeped. Ten seconds left.

"Turn your head a little and look past me," he directed. I did so and he laid his right arm behind my head. The camera beeped. Five seconds left.

He framed my face with his left arm and kissed my cheek. My eyes blinked and I grinned slightly. The camera snapped.

"See. That wasn't so bad," Miles laughed.

"You are one weird bird," I said, laughing, yet very serious.

"You're a good sport," Miles said. He slowly brought his leg back across the front of my body, hitting my erection on the way.

"Oh, my bad, I think I hit your phone," he said.

"Nah, my phone's on the couch," I said sheepishly.

"Oh. Was that?"

"My dick? Yeah." I stood and tried to flatten out my pants without Miles seeing.

"You on hard? Oh shit, I'm sorry."

"What are you sorry for?"

"I just...I didn't...I mean..."

"Oh, now you're at a loss for words?"

"Eustace, I'm sorry. This is awkward."

"*Now* it's awkward? It wasn't awkward when you took all your clothes off and showed me ya twig and berries?"

"I ain't think you were gonna get excited by me."

"Miles! I'm gay! That's what gay men do! We get turned on by naked men, just like a straight dude is gonna get turned on by a naked woman."

"But we're friends, though."

"Yeah, but you're still naked."

"I'm sorry, I really should have thought this through. I'll go put my clothes on."

"Please do." I walked to the camera and took it off the tripod. The picture probably wasn't shit anyway. With no preparation and hardly even a second thought about the lighting, I knew it wouldn't be my best work.

I looked at the digital display on the back and was astonished at what I saw.

"Miles!" I called.

"Yeah?"

"Get your ass out here!"

He rushed out of the bathroom wearing his black boxer briefs and sleeveless t-shirt.

"Look at this," I held the camera out and he stood beside me, looking at what I saw: a beautiful replica of one of the most iconic images of the seventies, but with a twist. A beautiful, African American man, naked as a jaybird, baring himself wholly to his friend, partner, or lover—who could really tell from the photo? But in that moment, the other man, the clothed man—me—was just as happy to be there as the naked man. Somehow, Miles had captured in that one moment everything there was to know about our relationship. His blissful ignorance. My restraint.

"This is beautiful, Eustace. See? I knew you could do it."

"Thanks for bringing it all together, Miles."

"Eustace? I should have talked to you about it first. I didn't even consider that you…you know…"

"Yeah. It's cool."

"Hey man, are you attracted to me?" he asked directly.

"That doesn't make a difference," I said coolly.

"Well, it does. To me. I don't want to take advantage of our relationship in any way, and I don't want to ever be misunderstood. I always get misunderstood."

"You? Misunderstood? No."

"Funny. So what's the answer?"

"Yes. Yes, I find you attractive. I find you very attractive."

"Wow. Wow."

"Well you certainly know you're a handsome dude."

"I don't know, I don't think of myself in that way. But more importantly, I'm very straight. I hope that doesn't complicate things between us."

"No, no, of course not. Nothing changes."

"Good. I like our friendship the way it is. I don't want to lose it just because I don't...you know...want to have sex with you."

"Miles. We're good. For real."

"And anyway, I thought you were with JJ."

"What! Why would you think that?"

"Well, aren't you with him?"

"No, we're just friends. He's not gay."

"You sure about that? He seems like he's really into you or something."

"Trust me. Me and JJ are not a thing. Never will be. I have mad love for him, but no."

"That's interesting."

"I mean he might say the same thing about you. I can't lie man, I've always thought the possibility was there."

"I get that a lot. I'm just really gay-friendly. Never made me a difference."

"You're real special, you know that?"

"Like crazy? Yeah, I know. I'm wired differently."

"You might be, but you don't miss a beat. I like that. And I like you, in spite of you being straight."

"You make it sound like it's a bad thing," he laughed.

"Nah. Only bad for me. But you'll make a woman truly happy someday."

"And you'll make JJ truly happy someday."

"Miles!"

"I'm sorry, but that dude is in love with you! Ray Charles could see that!"

"Miles…"

"Okay, okay. I'll stop."

"Put your clothes on. I'm going to upload these photos."

"You did good, man. I'm looking forward to seeing how the rest of the pictures come out."

I inhaled and exhaled. This was the craziest day ever, but one of the most artistically productive days of my early career. However, if Miles was going to be pledging a graduate chapter of my frat, and I wanted to keep my membership, our intimate photo would have to stay under wraps until after he crossed.

Dear Julian,

I've been working with an emerging model here in DC, trying to hone my craft even further. Take a look.

Regards,
Eustace

Dear Eustace,

I saw the new pictures as soon as you uploaded them to your site—I follow your career closely. Damn. So hot.

One day, we're going to work together again. I want to look as great as your models.

One love.
Julian

Chapter Three:
Late August 2005

Greetings Dean Big Brother Lamar, aka Juggernaut,
Number Eight, Alpha Chapter, Spring '96!

Greetings Big Brother Steven, aka The Good Son,
Number Five, Sigma Chapter, Spring '97!

Greetings Big Brother Jeremy Jacob, aka Caesar,
Number Two, Alpha Chapter, Spring '99!

Greetings Big Brother Micah, aka Abacus,
Number Three, Sigma Chapter, Spring '99!

Greetings Big Brother Angel, aka Morpheus,
Number One, Sigma Chapter, Spring 2000!

Greetings Big Brother Christopher, aka Moses,
Number Eight, Sigma Chapter, Spring 2000!

Greetings Big Brother Morris, aka Cruel Intentions,
Number One, Sigma Chapter, Spring 2001!

Greetings Big Brother Eustace, aka Hades,
Number Four, Beta Chapter, Spring 2001!

"Pledges, why are you here?" Lamar asked the line of three young black men.

"We are here to fully experience the bonds of brotherhood; to test our intellectual acumen; and to learn the facts, the legends, and the history of Beta Chi Phi Fraternity, Innnnnncorporated!"

"Why are you dressed in all black?" he asked.

"Black represents the unknown, and our trust and faith that you, Big Brothers, will lead us through the darkness into the light of Beta Chi Phi Fraternity, Innnnnncorporated!"

Miles was the tallest pledge, the tail of the line of three. He executed his responses perfectly.

"Why are the Big Brothers assembled before you?"

"You are here because you care; because you would never, ever let us join this fraternity without the proper foundation; and because our successful journey relies on the support of those who came before!"

"Will we ever hurt you?"

"Never, Big Brothers!"

"If that's true, why isn't all of the DC Alumni Chapter here with you tonight?"

"We love and respect every member of the chapter who would vote favorably upon us, and we respect the service and professionalism of DCAC; however, a middle ground must be sought between the old ways and the new ways. Therefore, we are led by you into the dawn of a new era."

"In other words?"

"In other words, some rules are made to be broken, Big Brother!"

Perfect, I thought. Sigma Chapter was a jewel in the crown of Beta's oldest chapters and easily the strongest in the DC area. If a man was to be properly made a Beta, authentically pledged in a spirit of love and brotherhood, it was widely known that Sigma Chapter was who you needed to come through in some way, shape, or form. If nobody from Sigma had been present in your process in this town, you might as well not be a Beta at all.

Alumni candidates were no exception. Sigma Chapter's local alumni presence stood at the ready to execute their take on the pledge process. Of course, this process was unsanctioned and technically against the rules of the fraternity. But the boys from Potomac University and Rock Creek College had good reason to believe in their version of the process.

"Pledges, please have a seat. I have a story for you." Christopher said. He was a tall, caramel brown brother with short, kinky hair. He had broad shoulders, a narrow waist, and a New York City swagger.

We, the Big Brothers, sat on the sofas and bar stools in Lamar's basement. The pledges sat comfortably on the floor, looking up at us in rapt attention. Of the three, Miles was the stiffest, an android sent from the future to carefully observe alumni pledging practices. It was good for him that he showed no emotion, as a pledge was supposed to be a clean slate anyway, with knowledge and traditions poured into him like an empty vessel.

Christopher sat directly in front of them while we listened.

"I pledged five years ago, Little Brothers. I was on the Spring 2000 line—The Phantoms. We were one of the largest lines in Sigma Chapter, in recent years at least. And that was one of our problems. Our chapter got big real quick. And not everybody who made it on our line by national standards was well known to the chapter. But they made it anyway and the chapter gave them a chance.

"About half of us had been groomed by the chapter. And we had great prophytes. I was lucky enough to have one of the best— Adrian Collins."

The faces of the pledges lit up. Adrian was the pride of Beta.

"You know Adrian. You haven't met him yet, but he is as awesome as everyone says. He's my spesh. Now he wasn't perfect— not by a longshot. But he tried his hardest to get things right. And he is one of reasons that Sigma Chapter is what it is today.

"Check it: In Spring 2000, my line of nine was coming through. It was a crazy process, but everybody's process was crazy. You're going to think your process is crazy. So it wasn't really a remarkable kind of crazy. But suddenly, it stops. The chapter got suspended after five weeks. We all get cease and desist letters. Luckily, we could continue with the workshops and ceremonies, but our prophytes were all banned from seeing us, pledging us, communicating with us. They weren't even invited to the official shit!

"We went nuts. They wouldn't return our calls or texts. They ignored us when they saw us in the street. We thought we fucked up big time.

"But my line brothers got cash together and put me on a bus to New York during spring break. We all knew he'd be at the tournament at Madison Square Garden, and if I could intercept him, I could find out what was going on and what we could do.

"The plan—crazy as it was—worked. I found him and convinced him to talk to me. He told me that it wasn't us, it was our grad advisor who was coming for us. That man always seemed like he hated us. To this day, I don't know why someone would be an advisor if they hate undergrads.

"But that wasn't the most meaningful part of us talking. That night was important because Adrian came out to me. I mean, we all pretty much knew it, but I'm the type of dude who doesn't believe anything unless I see it for myself. And when he told me…I don't know man, I felt honored. It's not easy being a gay black man in this world, but Adrian had this confidence. It's like…he insisted on being himself. And real talk, I can see why a dude like Isaiah Aiken would risk it all to be with him. It's like, you can be around Adrian and know something dope is about to happen.

"Anyway, something dope actually did happen: Adrian saved the chapter. Because of his relationship with Isaiah, he knew this lawyer lady. She used to work for Potomac, but she took on Sigma Chapter as a *pro bono* client. On the day of the formal investigation, this lady walks into the hotel suite with the regional director and tells him to take us off suspension—*tells him!* Like, can you imagine?

"And you know what the region director did? He took us off suspension! And we been unfuckwittable ever since."

"But…" Micah interjected. "That's the legend. It's based in facts, of course. And Adrian deserves praise for a lot of reasons. His pledging—our pledging—was tough. He considered dropping line when he was outed to the chapter before he was ready. And the brothers of the chapter, some of them treated him terribly. Harassment, during and after the process. Even physical violence. But he pushed through. Because of Adrian, and brothers like him, Beta Chi Phi is the kind of fraternity that's unafraid to look beyond a man's sexual orientation. We simply don't care who you love. We will gladly serenade your boyfriend, if you want us to."

"And many of us did. We literally sang our sweetheart song to him and his husband at their wedding reception. That was for Adrian. That's for who he is to us," Christopher continued. "And maybe one day you'll meet him. And brothers like him, like Mohammed Bilal, who never once agreed with the hazing and brutality we used to be known for. He stuck with us, too, and made sure that he was around to help develop a pledge process that we could live with—the one that you have today. We will never hit you and we will never bullshit you. Yes, we bend the rules, and we know we're not supposed to. But we believe that this is the best way to instill these values and to teach these traditions. We will always be the storytellers and the gatekeepers. And if there is one lesson to be learned about Beta Chi Phi, at least when it comes to the brothers that you will meet on this journey: When it comes to hazing, we off that."

For a moment, I saw a wave of wonder wash over Miles' face. As soon as I noticed that he was having a human emotion, he straightened into his stance of razor sharp focus.

I was happy enough knowing the lesson had been learned.

The night continued with more stories of brothers who weren't present but had been instrumental in the changing culture of the fraternity. There would always be chapters who pledged underground, and there would always be those chapters for whom swinging wood never went out of style. Yet there was hope that the men in this small pocket of the Beta nation would affect a paradigm shift that could transcend the negative parts of the culture.

I was proud to be among those men, and prouder to write Miles' letter of recommendation for the DC Alumni Chapter. JJ, too, wrote a supporting letter.

"Your boy's doing good," JJ whispered to me during a break in the evening.

"He's a fucking human computer is what he is," I mused. "I want him to mess up one good time so that we can see what he's really made of."

"He will. They all do, eventually."

I looked into JJ's eyes.

"You never struck me as someone who would admit a fault."

"They all mess up. *They*. Not me. I was perfect."

"You? The perfect pledge? Nigga please. If Lamar wasn't in the other room with the boys, I'd ask him about you."

"Please don't."

"Then tell me. Your biggest fuck-up while on line. Now."

"Okay, okay. So…I was supposed to be at set one night, and I completely skipped it to be with Sylvia."

It took every molecule in my body and the blood of Jesus to keep me from rolling my eyes at the thought of him being with that woman.

"I told them I was sick. Nobody knew the truth, not even my line brothers. The next night, when I did show up, I had all these hickeys on my neck. They gave me the blues. Not only did I take strokes, but my line name was almost 'The Town Slut.'"

I instantly and obnoxiously guffawed.

"That would have been *terrible!*" I chuckled.

"And it would have served me right."

"Thank God it didn't stick. 'Caesar' is more regal."

"Yo…you trying to do something after this is over?"

"Like what? Hit a club?"

"Nah. Hang out. My place."

"I don't know, JJ."

"It's right around the corner. Literally."

"JJ…"

"Just for a minute."

"Okay, JJ."

I never understood what it was about him that inevitably led to me making poor decisions.

At about one in the morning, the pledges had been dismissed and JJ and I were the first to exit Lamar's place in Southeast DC, in a neighborhood that looked remarkably like others in more affluent locations in the city, but blacker. JJ truly did live right around the corner in a garden apartment, in a sizable unit that he couldn't have afforded if it was closer to Georgetown Law.

We entered the building and my nostrils filled with that universal apartment hallway smell that was about one gym sock away from being called stench. We walked quickly, up the stairs and to the second floor.

"I don't think I've seen this place since you moved in," I said.

"Cuz you be fakin'," he replied.

The corner of my mouth clenched into a smirk, but I remained silent. I wouldn't be further baited by him tonight.

He swung the door open. The one-bedroom apartment looked largely as it had when he moved in: sparse furniture, including a large black sofa; a Beta paddle in the corner, leaning against black bookcases; a big screen television; and stools at a bar separating the kitchen from the living area.

"Sit down," he said. I took to the couch while he turned the air conditioning on. The soft hum filled the room quicker than the cool air. I patted the light sweat on my forehead which had accumulated in the heat of the August air.

"You want a drink?" he asked from the kitchen.

"I'm good. Not really in a drinking mood. Set has me thinking."

"Cool. No beer. What about water?"

"I could do water, thanks."

He emerged from the kitchen with two cold bottles of store brand water.

"Cheers," he said, tapping his bottle against mine. A few quiet minutes passed.

"So what happened in set that has you thinking?" he asked.

"Everything. The way we teach. The way we share information. The stories. The emotion. And we've always done things this way. At least for the chapters like ours. Sigma. Beta. Alpha."

"True, true. In the true African tradition."

"Yeah, I guess. But like...I wish I could photograph set."

"You know you can't do that."

"I know. But still, imagine what it would be like to see yourself at set. Would you recognize yourself? And how would you behave if you knew you would see yourself again someday?"

"I don't know. That's a good question, though."

"I had some fantastic prophytes, too. I mean, I didn't have no Adrian or Mohammed like Sigma Chapter, but I had some smart dudes in my corner. Me being gay was never a concern to them. I was never treated differently. I didn't go through anything that Adrian went through."

"You had your own journey, though. Still do."

"We all do. But I think about who I was then, who I am now, and how far I have to go before I become who I want to be."

"Who do you want to be?"

I stopped talking and looked at the door.

"I should go."

"Stay. It's very late and you're in Southeast DC."

"It's not a long walk to the Green line from here."

"Is Metro even running?"

"I'll catch a taxi."

"Stop running."

"I'm not running. I'm not. Really. I just...this isn't..."

"Stay." He took my hand and interlaced his fingers with mine.

"This isn't what you want, JJ. You know it."

"I can't explain to you what I want. And if I could, you'd never agree."

I tried hard to ignore him. I tried with every cell in my body.

"Tell me, Eustace. Who do you want to be?"

"I want..." I looked at him and froze. Beside me sat a man that I feared, that I loved, that I wanted every day of my life for the past four years. I knew that this would be a moment that I would remember for the rest of my life. I didn't need a camera to capture the memory. Every hair in his goatee, every eyelash, every pore in his skin, each curve in his eyebrows, the shine in his scalp, the slow heave of his chest, the light scent of his deodorant, the gleam of his teeth—every single physical and metaphysical pixel that created Jeremy Jacob Carter's image in my mind was trapped there forever.

"I want to be yours." I raised his hand to my lips and kissed it.

"Mine?" he smiled. "All mine?"

He leaned close to me, grinning all the while.

"You promise? You pinky swear promise? You get to be all mine?"

He pecked me quickly on the lips.

"Yes, I want to be yours. But you'll never be all mine."

His grin never disappeared.

"I can be...tonight."

He released my hand and quickly removed his Jordans. He stood before me as I sat. He took off his t-shirt and revealed his well-defined torso. His six pack was divided evenly by a faint trail of hair leading to the middle of his chest, where it stopped. His pecs, strong and broad, were accentuated by his deep brown nipples, already erect.

"I am all yours. All of me."

He unbuckled his leather belt, removed it, and let it fall to the floor with a thud. His khaki cargo shorts sagged low on his hips. He unbuttoned them, then unzipped the fly. They fell to the floor and he stepped out of them. He quickly pulled off his socks.

He stood before me in nothing but white boxer shorts with arms arrogantly folded.

I swallowed and spoke.

"All of you?"

He slowly nodded.

"All of me," he replied. He unfolded his arms and let his fingers slowly slide over his abs as they found their way to the band of his underwear. He bent over as he removed the final article. He stood straight up, revealing his semi-hard penis.

I sat in silence with my hands on my lap, entranced by his body and his admission.

"All of you?" I repeated. He nodded, walking slowly toward me. I licked my lips.

He straddled me as I sat on the sofa. I moved my arms from my lap to his waist. He was hot to the touch. I looked up at him. Still smiling.

I finally smiled back. He laughed.

"Be mine tonight. Okay?" he asked.

"Okay." I raised my chin. He leaned down and kissed me passionately. His tongue sought to know every piece of my mouth. I forgot to breathe.

He took my shirt off as we kissed. He looked amazed. My time in the gym had paid off, at least when it came to JJ. My smooth, dark chest and abs were his playground now. I continued kissing him, my mouth soon finding his neck and making a home there.

His penis, now fully erect, rubbed against my abs. He rolled his hips toward me in a slow rhythm and I thrust my still clothed bottom half back into him. He moaned.

"Hold on," I instructed. He held me tight and I stood up straight. He wrapped his legs around me as I quickly undid my belt and let my own shorts fall. My boxer briefs followed.

I adjusted myself so that my own penis was against his. I held him with one arm and used the other for balance as I laid him back on the couch.

His hands explored my body, from my back to my ass. He grabbed me there and held on for dear life as I continued kissing him and grinding him down into the couch. His breathing became more rapid and his groans stronger. I continued my intensive grind.

"Don't stop," he whispered in my ear. I kept the friction going between our two hard dicks and the slickness of pre-cum became our lubricant.

"Shit nigga, this feels so good," he moaned.

"Give me all of you, Jeremy Jacob," I whispered.

"Shit, my nigga. Shit, goddamn. I'm about to come."

"What?"

"Ah! Fuck, I'm cumming!"

I raised my body off JJ in time to see his immense, hard dick spurt semen all over his abdomen. I grabbed his dick and he yelped as I jacked him for the last few spurts.

"I'm sorry, Eustace. This never happens to me."

"It's all good. It happens to the best of us."

Ain't this about a bitch, I thought to myself.

"That was the best shit I ever felt, though," he continued.

"Ever?" I asked.

"Pretty sure," he said. His eyes closed.

"I'll get you a towel…or a washcloth…or something." I rose from between his legs and off his sofa.

"Thank you," he said. He repeated his thanks after I cleaned him off. He hugged me from behind as we walked, nude, from the sofa to his bedroom. As we got comfortable under the sheets, he turned away from me and wrapped my arms around him, settling into a spoon position with my chin on the top of his head.

"For real, yo…I ain't never come like that before," he reiterated for the record.

I smiled silently.

"Next time, you gonna let me get mine?" I asked. He nodded his head.

"Next time, like in ten minutes, right?" he asked.

"Ten minutes. Tomorrow. Next week. Whenever, Jeremy Jacob."

My hard penis rubbed against she small of his back and he pressed hard against me.

"You got me whenever, my dude. Wherever. However."

"Promise?"

"Pinky swear promise. I love you."

"I love you more," I said.

Soon, we'd drift off to sleep.

For the entirety of Miles' pledge process, and even some weeks thereafter, JJ and I played this game. We'd resist, then we'd succumb. We'd hold our breaths, then we'd exhale. We'd edge, then we'd climax magnificently—all over each other if need be—to feel that we were alive in those moments and those spaces where real life felt too real.

It was as toxic as a relationship could be without being physically abusive. I had a man who I knew I could never have. And I wanted to be a man that I knew I could never be. But in those moments and in those days in 2005, I could be everything that one man needed me to be, and he could be everything I needed him to be, at least when the lights went out.

Dear Eustace Dailey,

You there? Haven't heard from you in a little while. My album drops in a few weeks. I can't believe it's finally here.

You got cable? Catch me on 106 and Park. I'll be a guest on the day the album comes out.

I may be in DC shortly after that. My team is making the arrangements now.

One love.
Julian

Dear Julian,

Things have been busy on my end. Congrats on all your success! Let me know when you're in town.

Eustace

Chapter Four:
Late October 2005

Autumn came as quickly as JJ. Before I knew it, Halloween—and the end of Miles' pledge process—were almost upon us.

Since he was otherwise occupied, my weekends were filled with photography gigs with new models. None were as creative as Miles was, but it was nice stacking the extra cash.

I was always a simple dude. I wasn't a tightwad by any means, and I spent money where it was worth it to me, like rent on a convenient apartment above the Metro station or cutting-edge camera equipment. But I wasn't moved by collecting things aside from my own artwork.

Even though I had a license, I didn't have a car, either. DC was a walkable city that had reliable public transportation. Plus, anywhere I went, my brothers with cars were likely driving there.

So my money stacked while I watched. Eventually, I reached out to Adrian to get his advice on how I should make my money work for me. He referred me to Rebecca Templeton, the "lawyer lady" who helped save Sigma Chapter, who referred me to an investment manager that she trusted. I didn't even miss the money he invested, even though I hadn't decided on any long-term goals yet. I told him that I supposed I wanted a house someday, but that wasn't the whole truth.

In fact, I wasn't sure where I would even be living in a year, or whether I'd be doing the same work, much less ready to commit to buying a house. I hadn't heard back yet from the sole graduate program to which I'd applied but moving to New Mexico was so unlikely that I barely even thought about that application anymore.

Work was work. I did it. I smiled during the day. I made nice with my coworkers. Nothing about the job inspired me, but at least it gave me someplace to be when everyone else was at their own jobs.

When I wasn't working and shooting, I was in the gym, keeping my body tight. It was immensely easier to stay in shape as a working adult than it was in college. Although I hated being on a schedule, I loved that I had one. As much as I'd rather be having an adventure anywhere but in DC, the fact that I knew what time I needed to get up, eat, and sleep every day made it easy for me to keep my body in tip-top shape.

Knowing that JJ was seeing my body every weekend was added motivation. Our bizarre relationship grew even more absurd with the addition of intimate touch. We'd support Miles at set, then retreat to his apartment, fuck around, and sleep.

The most surreal part was that we never had anal sex during those days. Without question, I had been around the block a few times, but I knew JJ had not. Being together, jerking each other off, massaging one another, kissing deeply, and occasionally oral sex—all of that was on the table. And more often than not, JJ was content to fall asleep in my arms.

But anal? That was special. That involved a level of negotiation that I didn't think either of us was ready for. I was versatile in my position preference, but I leaned toward being a top. As for JJ, he hadn't decided yet, and I was in no hurry to force the situation.

He liked me. Being safe in my arms was all he cared about.

Toward the end of October, the date of Miles' initiation had finally arrived. The Brothers of the "underground railroad" of pledging had prepared him and his two line brothers as best we could for a lifetime commitment to our fraternity. In a thoughtful, if not sanitized way, we had instilled in them the most important values and beliefs of our brotherhood—and we did it without once hitting them. Regardless, it was a rigorous experience that they would not soon forget.

As Beta always had sunrise initiation ceremonies, JJ and I got dressed in the darkest hours of night, well before the sun rose. He was unusually quiet.

"I'm glad this is over for him," I said.

"Mmm-hmm. He worked hard. Never disappointed me once," JJ responded. We both stood in the bathroom mirror, tying our neckties and straightening our lapels.

"He's his own worst critic. He called me a few times, you know."

"Oh yeah?"

"Yeah. Always apologizing about something or another, things I would have never noticed. Like if he stumbled over a poem."

"Never peeped that."

"Nah. Me, either. Listen…you okay?"

JJ tightened the knot on his burgundy and gold striped necktie and put his hands on the vanity.

"Sylvia's coming to the crossing party tonight."

"Oh."

"I haven't seen her in months, you know."

"I know."

"Yeah…so…"

"It's Miles' night. What do I care about Sylvia being there?"

"I just wanted to let you know."

"Okay. So now I know."

I tried hard not to seethe. I tried to remember how to not give a fuck.

"I love you," he said.

"Oh, just shut the fuck up." I stormed out the bathroom, grabbing my fraternity pin and lion ring on the way out. I jammed the ring on my finger and hurriedly affixed the pin to my lapel.

He sauntered out the bathroom and casually gathered his wrist watch, class ring, and fraternity pin.

"I'm ready if you are," he said, looking me dead in the eyes.

I nodded and looked away.

We rode in silence from Southeast all the way to the Embassy Suites in Chevy Chase, where our ceremonies would be held. In that time, I got my shit together emotionally and got ready to welcome Miles into the fold. I hadn't muttered a word to him—or anybody—about what was going on between me and JJ.

We parked in the lot beneath the hotel and quickly found our way to the hotel elevator. The doors opened and we stepped in. The whole elevator car was mirrored on the inside.

"Damn. We look good," he said, staring at our reflections. I looked to the floor.

Dozens of Brothers were in the hotel lobby already, chit-chatting with one another and catching up on old times. JJ and I quickly separated. He found some Alpha Chapter prophytes of his from Boston University and Boston College, and I found my way to the DC Alumni Chapter leaders, asking how I could be of assistance.

I was directed to the ritual room, where I helped arrange the various ceremony stations in silence. I tried hard to disassociate myself from the feelings I was having regarding Sylvia's imminent appearance later that day.

Why was I so stupid?

"Hey, baby bro," a soft voice said behind me as he touched my shoulder. I quickly turned around.

"Adrian!" I exclaimed.

"What's up!" he howled. We embraced and held each other for a long time.

"I missed you, man! I had no idea you were coming."

"Surprise, bitch!" he chuckled.

"I'm so glad you're here. You are going to really like Miles."

"So I hear!" He smiled widely. I stood back and looked at him.

"Adrian, have you been working out? Jesus, you look ripped under that suit!"

"Yeah, a little bit, when I have time!"

"You been in the gym every day. Stop lying."

"Aight, you got me," he laughed. "For real, I've got a lot more free time since I quit working for that after school program."

"That's right, you did leave that job."

"Yeah. And Isaiah wants me to take care of Zion and establish our family foundation. And now that Zion's five, I don't even have a whole lot to do for him. He goes to school and is like 'fuck you, Papa, I got this now.' Little asshole."

We laughed.

"But you love that little asshole."

"I do, man. I never thought I'd feel this way about somebody else's kid."

"God bless you. That's a feeling I hope I never have!"

We laughed more.

"You're young, bro. You never know what life's going to throw at you. I wasn't even a senior in college when we found out about Zion. Now here I am."

"I know, bro. But you and me...we're different breeds. I can't do what you do."

"Aww...I hear you."

"Listen, I would love for you to stand with me and JJ when I pin Miles."

"I would be honored. I can't wait to meet him."

We buzzed around the room, arranging flowers here and aligning candles there, until the ceremony began. Brothers filed into the room first, then soon-to-be brothers were led in, blindfolded, by their official membership intake director. Their actual Dean, Lamar, was nearby as well. There wasn't a single person involved in their underground process who wasn't also an active and financial fraternity member. We didn't play around with Beta. If we were going to lead you into this fraternity, we were going to lead by example.

The ceremony, as it always is, was a beautiful display of our most sacred traditions. At the appropriate time, Miles turned around and was greeted by the men welcoming him into the frat. Adrian stood behind me, to the left, while JJ stood off to my right. I pinned him, showed him the fraternity handshake, whispered the password, and gave him a long, tight hug. He beamed with pride and with excitement.

The ceremony ended and we exited to another room, where a sumptuous breakfast awaited us all—as were tables filled with gifts for the new members. The three neophytes were stunned. The piles and piles of gifts practically reached the ceiling. Many gifts came from the eight men who had "seen" the three men when they were pledging behind closed doors. It is often said that the best gifts come from those who are the hardest on you, and we were no exception.

Miles came to his gift table, adorned with a sign which said "Brother Miles Johnson, #3-DCAC-Fall 05, 'Round About Midnight.'" Although we all had a hand in naming the new Brothers, it was truthfully JJ who had the most influence. He sought a Miles Davis album name, in homage to his real name, but one which also had something to do with his process. The album 'Round About Midnight was chosen because, as JJ said, that was the time that Miles showed any emotion whatsoever.

But today, Miles was all smiles. Adrian, JJ, Micah, Christopher and I surrounded him as he dug through the gift bags. Christopher's contribution was a messenger bag filled with all those Beta essentials like pens, a portfolio, and a lanyard. Adrian gifted him with a handmade paddle. JJ's present was a picture frame, personalized with his crossing information. And my gift was a burgundy varsity sweater with gold letters—just in time for the winter months.

Miles struggled finding the words.

"Wow. I'm overwhelmed. Thank you so much, guys."

"We're not *guys*," JJ interrupted. "We're Brothers. Now and forever."

Miles shook JJ's hand and pulled him into a tight embrace.

"Thank you, Brothers," he said, fighting to speak through tears. We circled them both and gave them a group hug.

I sat next to Adrian at breakfast. JJ had once again separated from me, opting to sit with his Brothers from Alpha Chapter.

Adrian leaned in and spoke to me softly.

"So...you and JJ?" he asked.

I looked up from my grits and dead into Adrian's eyes.

"Is it that obvious?"

"The part that's obvious? That y'all are having a fight. But y'all have always been an old married couple, haven't you?"

"So you just gonna read me for filth early on a Saturday," I said. Adrian laughed.

"Hey, Eustace. I'm really glad you're my Brother."

"Thanks, Adrian. I feel the same way."

"I know we don't talk a lot, but I feel as close to you as I do Brothers from my chapter. And we'll always have a lot in common. I don't want to see you get hurt."

"Please don't overestimate JJ's power. He can't hurt me."

"You make him sound like a supervillain," Adrian laughed.

"Isn't he?" I laughed back.

"You love him dearly," Adrian said.

"I do. And I hate it."

"Listen, man. I'm not one for relationship advice. I got super lucky with Isaiah. We make it work, somehow. But when it comes to JJ, man. I don't know. I think you're...well...better than this."

I laid down my fork.

"You judging me, Big Brother?"

"No, not in the least. Like I said, I don't want you to get hurt. You are an excellent guy, worthy of somebody who can love you just as you are. If JJ can do that for you, great. But if he's not interested in leaving his...situation...then I can only give you one piece of advice."

"And that is?"

"Run."

I nodded in full understanding and agreement.

"Are you living the life that you want?" he asked. I shrugged.

"I'm checking the boxes. That's enough, right?"

"Has there been anybody? Besides JJ?"

"No. Just casual hook-ups every now and then."

"It's okay to take your time to figure it out. This married life shit…I don't know how many ways I can say it, but it is not easy in the slightest. Don't envy this life unless you're ready to work for it."

"I hear you. Thank you, Adrian."

"You're welcome, baby bro."

"And just so you know…had you and Isaiah not been damn-near engaged, I would have asked you on a date as soon as I met you."

Adrian blushed.

"I might have let you. Regardless, it's nice to have somebody in the frat that understands this lifestyle."

"It really is. Love you, bro."

"Love you, too."

The morning came to a conclusion and we went our separate ways, though most of us would reconvene later that evening for the crossing party at Renard's.

JJ and I met by the elevator in silence.

"Did you have a good time?" I asked him.

"I did. These things always reinvigorate me. You?"

The elevator doors opened and we got on.

"Yes. It was fun."

"You and Adrian seemed to have a good time."

"It's always great catching up with him." JJ nodded.

"I, uh…I can drop you off at your place. Then…"

"You've got to pick up Sylvia from the airport."

"Yes. I do."

"I understand."

We entered his car in silence and stayed that way for the twenty-minute ride to U Street. I stole glances at him throughout, but mainly focused my attention on the passing scenery outside my window. Another Washington autumn was passing me by.

He parked in front of my building and idled.

"You will be there tonight, won't you?" he asked.

"Yes. I wouldn't miss Miles' debut."

"Me neither. I hope you know that. I've got his back just as sure as I've got yours."

I looked at him and lightly laughed.

"Yeah. I know."

I leaned over, kissed him on the temple, and hurried out.

I walked down U Street toward the venue for the party, my black blazer hugging my shoulders all the way. I wasn't going far enough or slowly enough to need an overcoat, but my burgundy scarf was the perfect accent to my slim-fitting ensemble of black pants and black shirt, open at the collar. When Betas got together to celebrate, we had to do it with style.

The medium-sized club was the perfect location to publicly welcome our new members to the world. We didn't have traditional probate shows for our alumni members, but I was eager to see what our line of three had in store to present themselves. I had no part in the planning.

The place began to fill when I arrived—the neos would be entering in about ten minutes, so I was cutting it close. But I knew that. I wanted to be as far away from Sylvia and JJ as possible for the whole evening. This was Miles' night. I didn't want him to sense any friction between us.

Nina, Adrian, Micah, and other folks I knew had already staked out a table and saved me a seat. I kissed Nina on the cheek and gripped the Brothers. I ordered an Old Fashioned and quietly waited.

The chatter went on around me and I retreated into myself for a spell. Sipping my drink, the bourbon slowly warmed me from the inside. I looked around and tried to find reasons to be happy. I was in my element, after all, so why did I feel so empty?

I had my frat brothers here, even all my favorite ones. Nina was always the life of the party. Miles would come out soon. I had a beverage. I had my life.

And I felt like crying.

"You okay?" Adrian mouthed from across the table.

I smiled and nodded. Why had I ever told Adrian that I would have asked him out? Awkward. Those are words I'd never be able to take back. He could never see me the same way.

A voice from the club's sound system got our attention. "Ladies and gentlemen, please turn your attention to the dancefloor for a special presentation by the newest members of Beta Chi Phi Fraternity,

Innnnncorporated.   The Fall 2005 line—better known as the Triumvirate of Soul!"

The three men marched out while chanting a Beta song. They wore identical black slacks, black shoes, and burgundy dashikis with a faint gold overlay. Under the loose dashikis were gold long-sleeved, mock turtleneck shirts.

They looked as though they'd stepped right out of a 1970 yearbook. It was amazing. We went wild.

The men gave a fifteen minute performance. Far less a probate show, it was more like a step and stroll routine. Seeing Miles relaxed enough to perform an entire choreographed routine was an amazing experience from beginning to end.

Upon the conclusion of their routine, they called all the Brothers "to the floor" to join them in singing the fraternity hymn. I stood next to Miles. JJ, who I had not seen in the room until that moment, stood on the other side of the circle, smiling at Miles in acknowledgment.

My heart hurt. What was happening to me?

I hugged Miles and told him how proud I was of him, for the second time that day.

"I couldn't have done it without you," he said.

"I know," I joked, lightly punching his shoulder. I returned to the table, chugged the rest of my Old Fashioned, and ordered another.

"Have you eaten anything?" Nina asked.

"I had a little dinner earlier," I lied.

"Oh. Okay then."

She looked concerned. *I should just leave*, I thought. I stood and looked around, hoping to catch my server. I did, but she already had my drink in hand. I took it and remained standing, scanning the room.

There they were.

There *she* was. Seated at a cluster of sofas on the other side of the lounge, JJ sitting next to her, holding court among the other traveling brothers. Caesar knew how to hold the attention of his adoring followers.

Sylvia Gibbs was the perfect first lady to Caesar. Her posture was perfect. Her hair was laid. She laughed at his jokes. She knew all the brothers. She was dark and poised and beautiful and everything a man could want.

I downed the rest of my drink in seconds and slammed my glass down to the table.

Adrian and Nina looked up, startled.

"Sorry." I took a seat again. Miles came over to sit with me for a spell.

"So now that this is over, it's time for our photos to go public," he announced.

"Nigga what? Public?"

"Let's have an art show."

"Wait, wait. A whole art show? Like when?"

"Soon. In a few weeks. It's time."

"I'd have to order prints. Get easels. Find a space. All that. Naw, that's too much."

"It's not. Let's talk about it Monday. Lunch on me."

"Aight. Bet."

How many drinks had it been now? Enough to politely go say hello to Sylvia? How much time had it been?

Hail Caesar.

I stood up. Again. I sauntered across the dancefloor toward Sylvia and JJ. She and I locked eyes, and if I wasn't bugging out, I'm sure she shot me this look as though she was pleased with herself that it was *me* approaching *her*.

Wait a minute. Was this bitch playing games with me? I should lean in and whisper all those nasty things her man lets me do to him.

Old conservative ass divinity school ho.

"Sylvia!" I called. She and JJ looked up and smiled.

"Eustace Dailey!" she rose and greeted me, grabbing my hands and holding them out in between us.

Is this bitch giving me the Oprah hug?

"It's so good to see you," I said.

"You too! How's the photography?"

"It's coming along well, I'd say. I'm not shooting probate shows like I used to, but there are plenty of other things to capture."

"I bet there are."

"And how's divinity school so far?"

"Princeton is great!"

"Awesome!"

"Yes, and JJ is coming up to visit me next weekend—you should come, too! It would be great showing you around campus."

"Oh," I grimaced. "Unfortunately I have some work travel next weekend. You know how it is."

"That's too bad," she said.

"Indeed," I concluded. "Well, JJ, enjoy your trip. Sylvia—always a pleasure."

"Take care," she said.

"Sure. You as well."

Why hadn't JJ muttered a single word that whole time? I walked back toward my table, but Lamar and Christopher grabbed me and led me to the neos' table, where they were all about to do shots.

"Shots of what?" I asked.

"Fuck if I know! Just take it!" Lamar shouted over the din.

"B-Chi!" a neo led.

"Chi Phi!" we responded, taking the shots straight to the head. It was some sort of whiskey. It tasted terrible, but I wasn't in the business of good taste these days.

How many drinks was it now? How many should I take to celebrate being able to talk to—and even touch hands with—Sylvia Gibbs?

I had to pee.

I wandered my way to the men's room. The tiny room had red tile and a black metal stall separating the toilet from the urinal. It was empty and smelled clean, a first for me at a social event.

Why is it that you never know how drunk you are until you're standing at a urinal? I prayed to God I wouldn't suddenly pass out while I was peeing, fall backwards, get a concussion, and keep pissing myself while I was unconscious with a gash in my head. It'd be just my luck to bleed out with my dick out.

I finished, shook it, repacked it, and flushed. The door swished open as I turned around. Ignoring whoever had just entered, I lathered my hands with soap and rinsed them off. I tore off a handful of paper towels, dried off, and prepared to leave. Whoever entered stood in my way.

"'Scuse me, homes," I said.

"No," JJ replied. I looked up.

"Oh. It's you."

"Are you okay?"

"Uh, yeah. Are you okay?"

"I'm fine."

"Oh, you're fine. Sylvia's here and all is right with the world. You are such a fucking E. Lynn Harris novel."

"E. Lynn…nigga, fuck you!"

"No, fuck *you*. And get out of my way."

"Make me, nigga."

I shoved the ever-loving shit out of JJ, pushing him against the men's room door. I grabbed him by the collar and hissed.

"We are not doing this here. Leave me the fuck alone."

He reached his hand to my crotch and rubbed it.

"Give me this," he commanded. The alcohol on his breath was as strong as mine. He kept rubbing me through my slacks, making my hard-on grow stronger and stronger.

"We can't do this." He unzipped me anyway.

"We're doing this."

He pushed me into the open stall and closed it behind us. He unbuckled my belt, unbuttoned my pants, and pulled them and my underwear down to my ankles in one swoop. My dick sprang to attention and hit him in the chin. He grabbed it with his right hand and grabbed my ass cheek with the other.

I thrust almost the entire thing into his mouth and he softly gagged. I pulled back.

"You want this dick?" I asked.

"Yes," he said, in between slurps. I grabbed his head and guided myself carefully into his throat. I moaned softly.

I was too drunk to notice that the lock to the stall hadn't caught, so when Adrian walked in, we locked eyes instantly. JJ was too into the blowjob to look up or feel remotely ashamed. He was in the zone.

Adrian's eyes grew wide as he saw JJ attacking my erection. I smiled at him and closed the stall door, again, this time making sure the latch caught. I could hear him chuckling lightly as he relieved himself in the urinal next to us. He washed his hands and exited.

In a few more minutes, I was close to a climax.

"I'm gonna come, JJ."

He continued to suck, deep throating my dick. I gasped, then exhaled, coating his throat with my hot ejaculate. He slowly released my dick from his mouth and swallowed my load. He got to his feet and I fixed my clothing. We left the stall in silence.

"Hey," I said.

"What?"

"Kiss your bitch goodnight for me."

He threw me a middle finger and quickly rejoined the party. I looked in the mirror, straightened my tie, tucked in my shirt, and smirked.

Dear Julian,

Congratulations on your debut album! I saw you on 106 & Park and I bought the album the day it came out. It is absolutely fantastic.

Stay tuned. I've got some photography news for you.

Regards,
Eustace.

Dear Eustace Dailey,

I can't wait!

One love,
Julian

Chapter Five:
Early November 2005

"Aye Frat, it's amazing you even still have a liver after that night," Miles teased.

"Jesus. I am never going to drink again."

"Lies."

Miles treated me to lunch as he said he would on the Monday after he crossed. It was the least he could do, he explained, to repay me for leading him to the light, through a meaningful pledge process.

"But I wanna get these pictures shown, man. As soon as possible."

"What's the rush?" I asked, sipping my cranberry juice.

"Well, what I didn't tell you the other night is that Georgetown fashion week is coming in a few weeks."

"Georgetown has a fashion week? What about DC fashion week?"

"Two different events entirely. Georgetown fashion week is focused more on the *haute couture* side of the industry as well as the high concept photographers. It's really focused on the artistry of design, modeling, and photography. It's perfect for us."

"What did you have in mind?"

"Well, one of the stores at Georgetown Park Mall just closed. The space is empty—totally open. Like a white box. I happen to know a mall manager, and he said he'd be happy to host a one night, pop-up event highlighting your work."

"So wait…you pretty much already have this figured out?"

"Yep."

"And you pretty much did all this while you were pledging?"

"Yep."

"When did you have time?"

"'Round about midnight…" he quipped. I laughed heartily.

"Miles, I don't think I can get prints of my images that quickly, and all the other stuff we'd need."

"Then we scrap the prints. We got white walls—why don't we get some projectors and display your images that way?"

"People won't think that's cheap?"

"Throw some lasers and a disco ball up. It's high fashion."

"Lasers…and a disco ball…"

"Or something! Let's just do it, man!"

"Okay, fine, we'll do it. Tell your man at the mall we want the space. In two weeks, you said?"

"In two weeks."

"Let's do it."

While I scrambled to put together photos that fit the mood of the show that Miles would direct, JJ gallivanted across Princeton with his girlfriend. Facebook seemed to rub my face in a new picture every morning. Sylvia and JJ at the Princeton Chapel. Sylvia and JJ in front of ivy-covered columns at the Morven Museum and Garden. Sylvia and JJ at the Battle Monument. Sylvia and JJ in front of Nassau Hall.

I hoped they got calluses from all the walking.

While Miles handled the planning with the venue, I promoted the hell out of my first art show. Since I had to be on Facebook anyway to stalk JJ and Sylvia, I figured I might as well use the network to invite my circles to the show.

What's up, y'all? So great news: my neo Miles hooked me up with my first art show during Georgetown Fashion Week. I hope y'all can come through and show some love. I'm going to be displaying some never before seen images. The drinks will be flowing, so roll through!

I sent a similarly worded invitation through email. That was on a Wednesday morning. By Friday afternoon, 250 people had RSVPed. By the following Friday, that number had swelled to a thousand.

Miles was elated. I was nervous.

"Are there really a thousand people out there?" I asked Miles? I dabbed the sweat from my brow in the makeshift dressing room at the rear of the store. It was likely a break room in a previous life, or a manager's office. I picked up a cocktail Miles had brought me to calm my nerves.

"No, there aren't a thousand people. People RSVP on Facebook all the time, but never show."

"Oh."

"But there are a good 150 in the seats and another 150 waiting to get in. We should probably start the show so we can rotate people out."

"Yeah. That works."

A light tapping on the dressing room door caught my attention. Miles opened it.

"Hey Frat!" he said to JJ, gripping and embracing him.

I sighed and sipped the cocktail again. It was strong, like I needed my drinks these days.

"Hey Eustace," JJ said with a smile.

"Hey," I replied.

"I brought you these." He had a bouquet of yellow roses in his hand. I remained expressionless.

"Miles, I'll be out in three minutes. Cue the music, please."

"Gotcha. See you soon." He quickly departed.

"So good luck tonight," JJ said.

"What are you really doing?" I asked.

"I don't understand. I'm showing support. Like I always do. Thought you'd like the flowers."

"You ever seen flowers in my apartment?"

"No, but..."

"Thanks, though," I took the bouquet and placed it on the table.

"The show's about to start," I announced.

"Eustace...come on," JJ pleaded.

"Come on where? To what?"

"There's no need for all this."

"There's no need for the way I been feeling, either. But I feel it. Don't I?"

"I'm sorry."

"No you ain't. You always get what you want. Your life is always gonna look perfect."

"But you know it's not!"

"Nobody ever challenges you. It's always smooth sailing for you."

"If nobody challenges me, it's because you challenge me the most. That's why I-"

"Don't. Just don't."

"Eustace...Why does it seem like we hate each other?" he asked me.

"You hate me? Good. Maybe you should."

JJ's head dropped. My intro music played in the main room. It was the instrumental to Lil' Kim's "Kitty Box," a funky, rock-infused hip-hop track with a strong beat.

"I'm sorry I bothered you, man. I won't anymore."

"Enjoy the show, Frat."

JJ quickly left the room, and I followed. I waited in the hallway, listening to Miles' introduction over the DJ's beat.

"Ladies and gentlemen, the man you've been waiting for. Your favorite photographer's favorite photographer. Unsung and unsigned talent, right here in the Nation's Capital. Here in his first show, I'd like to introduce you to my friend—my Spesh—Mr. Eustace Dailey!"

I came out to roaring applause. The darkened room was filled with my friends, admirers, former clients, and complete strangers. Two runways divided the audience into four sections. On the runway's edges were four laptops connected to four projectors.

I stepped to the intersection and waved to the audience, who continued their ovation.

"Thank you so much for coming out. Many of you are already familiar with my work, but at the urging of my dear friend and fraternity brother, I thought it might be time to reintroduce you to who I am and what I'm all about. So relax, grab a drink, and enjoy this retrospective."

I took a seat in the front row and watched the show begin. The slideshows were synchronized so that no one screen overpowered the other.

On the screen flashed my many fraternity and sorority pictures, which faded into my landscapes and architectural photos. While the show continued, Miles' ushers passed out my business card to every visitor.

The music matched the show perfectly. As the landscapes flashed to my portraits, Mariah Carey and Snoop Dogg's "Say Somethin'" played. The men and women who modeled for me in the past were beautiful and perfectly posed in each shot. Although there were many images that didn't make it into the show, I was overwhelmed to see the dozens of great shots I had taken over the past few years.

Why *wasn't* I doing this full-time?

The final act displayed my more risqué shots, including many with Miles. With every striking shot of Miles that featured his haunting eyes, the crowd gasped and applauded.

The last image was the John Lennon/Yoko Ono re-creation, the only image in which Miles is fully nude and the only image which included me. The audience screamed and rose to their feet as all four slideshows ended on the image. I rose and waved as the images faded away, one by one, as the instrumental to "Don't Cha" by the Pussycat Dolls swelled to a crescendo.

JJ hurried from the room without looking back. I waved harder at my adoring fans, pointing to the folks that I knew and giving them thumbs up.

I shook the hands of everyone who had supported the event and made sure they knew the name of my new website: www.eustacedailey.com. Miles beamed, and I became warm on the inside. It felt good to be known for doing something well.

"I owe this all to you, man," I said to him before the second showing of my photos.

"It's the least I could do. Truly. Never forget that you're more than just a Beta to me—or anybody."

The following weekend was the last weekend before Thanksgiving. Right when Adrian, Isaiah, and Zion would be returning to town to spend time with Adrian's mother, the rest of the crew would be traveling away from DC to be with our own families. Even though DC was home, it wasn't where we were from.

The Betas had an annual pre-Thanksgiving fellowship brunch at a brother's spacious home in Northeast DC. The members of the chapter, inactive members, our friends, and our families were all invited to participate. It was often the last time we'd all see each other before the bustle of the winter months began.

There was no formal program and no expectation that any of us had to stay the whole time, yet the event often extended well past brunch hours and ended late into the evening.

I arrived alone with a bottle of wine in hand for our host, an older Brother from DCAC who had been made at the Lambda Chapter at Penn.

"Brother Dailey!" he exclaimed. "Thank you so much for coming. I'm surprised you had any availability these days!"

"Always got time for the frat," I smiled, handing him the bottle.

"Ooooh-wee, the good stuff! Thanks, Brother! Come on in, the gang's all here."

I walked slowly through the living room, waving at Brothers I had casually seen at chapter meetings. I wasn't well acquainted with the older Bros, but we were all friendly with each other. I was far more comfortable with the younger Brothers, who'd surely be in the kitchen or the fully furnished basement.

In the kitchen was a trashcan—clean, of course—of our fraternity's signature drink: Beta-ade. A deep, crimson concoction consisting of whatever clear alcohol was on hand and whatever juice could make it blood red, Beta-ade was a dangerous game.

I chugged my first cup before anyone else joined me. I poured my second cup and proceeded to the basement.

As I predicted, the younger brothers and their guests were already there. Adrian was there, with Zion seated in his lap with a small plate of bacon and eggs.

"This is not Zion!" I exclaimed.

"Uh huh!" Zion said back to me.

"Say hi to Mr. Eustace, Zion," Adrian said.

"Hi Mister Useless!"

"Eustace! Say Eustace, Zion!"

"Useless!"

I laughed until tears streamed from my eyes.

"That ain't the first or last time I'll be called useless!"

"How you doin'?" Adrian asked me.

"I'm good, bro."

"I heard your show was on fire."

"Sure was, man. It was perfect."

"Led to more gigs?"

"Lots. I'm taking my time, though. I got some irons in the fire and I'm not trying to take on any work but the work I really want."

"Irons in the fire?"

"Yeah. We'll see."

"You see who's here, right? Look around."

I turned around and saw Sylvia and JJ cozied up to one another on a piano bench. I turned back around sharply.

"Dude, if you rolled your eyes any harder, they would have popped out and rolled down South Dakota Avenue. Last time I saw y'all together, you looked satisfied and he looked...occupied."

"I'm not trying to go there with him today."

"Then don't. Live your life. It's a pretty good one, if you haven't noticed."

"Yeah. You're right." I finished my drink. Adrian looked concerned.

"What?" I asked

"You've been tossing them back pretty heavy these days."

"I always drink like this, man. Don't act brand new."

"Okay. I'm just saying."

"I'm fine, Adrian. Seriously. So how's Isaiah? Pretty good season so far, right?"

"Yeah, pretty good! But he's got the itch to move on. He wants a ring."

"Yeah, I can imagine. Is Nina coming today?"

"Nah, she and Micah went out of town."

"Micah? Your line brother?"

"Yeah...I guess they're trying to figure out what's next."

"Wow. Well good luck to them."

"Yeah...we'll see."

"Brothers! Friends...can I have your attention please?" JJ asked over the noise of the small crowd. He continued.

"Is Brother Jenkins down here? Good, good. Listen...there comes a time in every man's life where he's got to step up. Right? And I've been coming to these brunches every year since I started law school. Now, I got just about a semester left and I'll be moving on. Maybe I'll be in DC, maybe I'll be elsewhere. But I know that no matter where I go, two things will be constant. First, I will always have the love and support of my Brothers of Beta Chi Phi, no matter where I go. And second, I will always have the love and support of this woman, my girlfriend Sylvia Gibbs. No matter where I go, I want her to be there. And to ensure that, I'd like to ask her one thing."

He dropped to his knee, reached into his pocket, and produced a little black box.

"Sylvia Gibbs...will you marry me?"

The words echoed in my head infinitely.

I kinda wish we were living together.
Sweating. Dizzy.

I love that. Don't stop.
"Sylvia Gibbs…will you marry me?"

I could stay like this forever.
Nauseated. Sick.

There's no other place in this universe that I'd rather be right now than here next to you. Crazy, right?
I need to leave.

Of course I love you.
"Sylvia Gibbs…will you marry me?"

Don't you trust anybody?
My heart. My lungs. My blood.

Trust me.
I should have never trusted him.

I'm not gay. But sometimes you make me wish that I was.
"Sylvia Gibbs…will you marry me?"

Yes, I get fucking jealous when there's another guy in your life.
My Brother. My friend.

Give me this.
I am yours. All of me.
My love. My one and only.
"Sylvia Gibbs…will you marry me?"

"Yes! Absolutely!" Everyone assembled cheered, from little Zion to the Brothers to all the adult guests. I clapped. I smiled. I gazed upon the happy couple as they embraced. Brother after Brother approached them, patting JJ on the back.

It felt like slow motion, moving through the throng, just to touch JJ on the shoulder and squeeze him. He spoke to someone else, and as quickly as I had touched him, I'd pulled away, returning to the staircase. I felt him try to grab my arm, but I pulled away, focusing on getting the hell out.

I heard nothing. I saw nothing. I hurried away.

"See you, Brother Jenkins." I escaped his house through the front door. I ran half a block down the street, stopped at a tree, and vomited on the curb in between two cars.

I can't be his friend.

"Eustace, you good?" Miles' low tenor and quick footsteps echoed off the cold concrete behind me. I heaved and spewed into the street once more.

"Yeah, that's attractive," he quipped.

I coughed and threw up once more.

"Let it out. And take this napkin."

I reached my arm toward him and grabbed the paper napkin. I wiped my mouth.

"You been drinking a lot today?" he asked. I nodded. "Okay. Just lean on the tree until you're ready to talk."

I nodded again and stood with my butt against the tree and my hands on my knees for support.

"All things considered, you don't look too bad. That was quite a proposal, wasn't it?"

I put my finger in the air, gagged once more, and puked again into the street.

"Thought so," he said. Tears streamed from my face as I got the last bit of bile from my system.

"Eustace, you have to get it together," he said.

"You don't understand, Miles."

"No, I don't. I know I care about you, and I care about JJ, but let's face it man: he's a scoundrel."

"Who says 'scoundrel' in 2005?"

"Your neo does. He's a dirty, rotten scoundrel. He's a good brother. But he's a dog. How don't you see that, man?"

"I know he's a dog. But what does that make me?"

Miles shrugged.

"It makes you Eustace, I guess. Eustace Dailey. The brother. The photographer."

"I'm a dummy, that's what I am. A dummy who thought I could love that nigga into being what I needed him to be."

"You're not a dummy. You can't help who you love."

"But I sure could have helped acting on it, right? What a fucking cliché."

"Are you feeling better?"

"I'm okay. I'll walk down to the avenue and catch a cab home."

"Let me take you home."

"No. I need the air. I need to think. But...thank you, Miles. I appreciate you. Please tell Adrian I'll see him next time."

"Will do. Be safe, Frat."

Miles pulled me into his embrace. I had done absolutely nothing to deserve his brotherhood or friendship in this moment, yet I accepted his embrace anyway.

I was hurt, embarrassed, heartbroken, ashamed, guilty, angry. I wanted to fight. I wanted to cry. But most of all, I wanted to die.

Dear Eustace Dailey,

I read all about your show during Georgetown Fashion Week. You, sir, are epic. I am really happy for you. I can't wait for your next moves.

One love,
Julian

Dear Julian,

Thanks man. I appreciate your support.

Eustace

Dear Eustace Dailey,

Are you okay?

One love,
Julian

Dear Julian,

Not really.

Why do you always use my whole name when you write me?

Eustace

Dear Eustace Dailey,

Because your name is amazing. Don't you think so?

Is there anything I can do for you? For real.

One love,
Julian

Dear Julian,

It doesn't feel like an amazing name to me. It sounds like the name of an old white man.

I'm going home for Thanksgiving. St. Louis. I'll be okay. Don't worry about me.

Eustace

Dear Eustace Dailey,

When I think of the name Eustace Dailey, I remember one of my favorite live performances of my career so far. How this tipsy stranger got his shit together long enough to take dope photos and have a dope conversation with me.

Every time I type your name, it brings me to a happy place. So, Eustace Dailey, never think your name belongs to an ugly old white man. It belongs to you.

I hope you have a happy Thanksgiving. Seriously. Hit me up when you have time.

One love,
Julian

Chapter Six:
Thanksgiving 2005

To my utter disappointment, the plane back home to St. Louis had neither crashed in the mountains over West Virginia, nor into any body of water we passed over. It would have been simpler for God to take me home in a divinely ordered accident rather than hatch a plan to end my own life. Who wants to be the one to discover my body? At least the people who recover corpses after plane crashes are used to that.

Although I hadn't died, I didn't feel ready to live, either. I walked through baggage claim and waited for my suitcase to come around the carousel.

"Eustace Dailey?" a familiar voice asked. I hesitated, praying it wasn't who I thought, then turned around. Yep, it was him.

Antonio Broussard. Still tall. Still beautiful. Still a son of a bitch.

In the fall of 1997 at Metro Academic and Classical High School in Saint Louis, Missouri, I was the newly elected student body president, co-captain of the tennis team, photography editor for the yearbook, and co-founder of the gay-straight alliance. I usually got As on my report card, except for the occasional B in science or math. I didn't need to be valedictorian, but I knew I wanted to be in the top ten.

The only thing that could have been better about my teenage years was the extra weight I had. Perhaps about 15 to 20 pounds heavier than I wanted to be, I didn't work it off until I got to college. Until then, I was the happy-go-lucky and fluffy kid that everyone liked being around.

I loved life. I loved high school. I didn't have one of those tragic upbringings with unsupportive parents who kicked me out of the house at 14. When I came out to my parents, Shirley and Roderick Dailey, they joined PFLAG. I wasn't tormented and bullied when I came out at school. I was already popular and well-liked, so why flip the script? Coming out was just a sliver of my overall awesomeness.

I was so badass, in fact, that I "skipped my turn" when it came time for student body elections. It was unheard of for a junior to run for the office of president, but I'd been active in student council for my whole first two years at Metro, and before then in junior high. I had even attended a special leadership camp for other dorks like me in upstate New York. For me, at least, it was a no-brainer that I would put all the skills I'd learned to good use.

I ran against two seniors, Antonio Broussard and Tiffany Fontaine. Antonio, the light-skinned beanpole with braces, still had a masculine elegance about him. He had fine, curly hair and a prominent Adam's apple. I thought he was cute, in a dorky way, but he hated my guts. He served as vice president of student government when I was community service chairman. He had a lot of influence on whether my programs would get funded, and they usually were not.

He always had something slick to say about my clothing, whether it was too loose for his liking or too tight. He criticized the way I spoke—always properly, at least in school. And should I have the misfortune of running into him alone in a hallway, he wouldn't speak at all.

In therapy, my counselor told me that Antonio probably hated me because I was everything he couldn't be: out, proud, and confident.

I laughed. There was no chance in hell that Antonio was gay, much less jealous of me.

My therapist insisted, comparing Antonio to a schoolyard bully who torments the ones he secretly loves.

Now he was telling fairy tales. I ended therapy shortly after that.

Tiffany Fontaine was a nice enough girl. Petite, pretty, put-together. She had been the student council secretary. We got along well. I wasn't running *against* her, I was running *for* the office.

We drew straws when the time for speeches came. I went first, Tiffany went second, and Antonio went third. My mom had always told me to go first, if possible, because I would set a high bar that no one else could reach. I felt lucky.

I gave a rousing, three-minute speech about creating a Metro High that was truly for all students, especially those who felt like outsiders. I had a dream that one day, nerds and jocks, goth kids and cheerleaders, special ed kids and gifted kids, could one day live peacefully at a Metro that valued who they were, not where they came from and how they looked. I told them that hope was on the way. I told them we could make Metro great again.

I don't remember what I really said. But it was good. So good, in fact, that Tiffany struggled through her speech and Antonio failed to connect with the audience. He was even booed when he brought up my lack of experience because—and this was his fatal flaw—I was *just* a junior.

I came in first, Tiffany came in second, and Antonio came in a distant third. He was the shame of the senior class.

That afternoon, after school, Antonio confronted me at my locker.

"You think you're something special, don't you?" he asked, finger pointed in my face.

"I don't think it. I know it. Shouldn't everybody?" I shrugged, ignoring his tirade.

"This is all I had, Eustace, and you took it from me. You get everything!"

"That's not my problem, Antonio. You've been mean to me ever since you met me. What did I ever do to you besides try to plan some community service projects? Serves you right for being a fucking bully."

"You don't know shit about what I've been through."

"We all go through, Antonio, cry me a fucking river."

"You don't know shit!" he said, banging my locker shut.

"Hold up." Antonio's eyes welled with tears. "Are you…"

"I'm not crying."

"But you're about to." Before he turned away, I grabbed him and pulled him toward me.

"I'm sorry," he said. I hugged him. He broke down into sobs and his knees got weak. I squeezed him tight.

"I have been a real dick to you. And I'm sorry. You're gonna be a great president. I know it," he said.

"Thank you. Antonio, what's really going on?"

"I gotta go. Maybe we'll talk about it another time

Another time became the next week, when Antonio and I walked home together after school. We talked a lot—he had good ideas for the school's future that I wanted to discuss, and he was happy to. It was amazing what a humbling ass whooping during an election will do for one's character.

We got to my house and we stopped on the street before I walked up the porch steps.

"Well, good talking to you." He nodded, looked toward the roof of my house, and scratched his head. He grimaced and squinted an eye.

"Eustace, I have something to tell you."

"Go ahead. I'm listening." I leaned against the railing on the stairs of my front porch.

"My parents kicked me out."

"What? Why?" I asked. His head sank.

"Why do you think?" he asked. I looked at him. His brown eyes looked up at me as he thrust his hands into his jacket pockets.

"Really?" He nodded.

"They kicked me out because I'm like you are. I'm gay. I don't...I don't have a place to stay tonight. Or any night. I guess I'm homeless."

"Wow."

"What am I going to do?" he asked.

"You're going to come inside. We're going to ask my folks if you can stay here for a few nights. And then we'll see what's next."

"For real?"

"Yes, for real. Come on up."

We went inside and Antonio explained the situation to my parents. Shirley and Roderick were shocked that anyone could throw away their own flesh and blood, so they were happy to welcome Antonio into their home.

A few days became the whole school year. Antonio lived in my older sister's old bedroom and I lived next door. We went from mortal enemies to practically brothers overnight.

Seeing the real Antonio, the vulnerable Antonio, softened my heart that year. I quickly learned compassion and empathy because of him. He had been a jackass because he lived with jackasses who wanted him to be tough, but it wasn't who he was.

But that's why he didn't know whether to love me or hate me. I had that mental toughness that he wanted so desperately. I was tough enough to be black, gay, out, and proud at home and at school. He could be none of those things.

Around Christmastime, our feelings grew more than brotherly. Like I said, I always thought he was cute, but I never thought he felt the same way about me. I had a lot going for me, but confidence with dudes was not one of them.

Woods abutted my house, and about 25 feet into them, there was a clearing. I'd always played back there as a child, but the most special time was the year's first major snowfall. I took Antonio back there to visit for the first time.

"Aw man! This is cool!" he yelled.

"Isn't it?" I hurled a snowball straight to the side of his head, where it landed with a thud.

"Asshole!" he said, scooping a handful of freshly fallen snow while I ran away.

We had an epic snowball fight that afternoon. I landed a few. He landed a few. Finally, we called a truce and walked to the middle of the clearing.

"So it's over?" he asked.

"Never!" I said, clipping him at the legs. He fell into the snow with a laugh. He pulled me down with him and we tussled back and forth. He got the advantage and laid on top of me, pinning my hands above my head.

"Okay, you got it!" I laughed until my chest hurt. He looked at me strangely, like he had seen something he had never seen before.

"What?" I asked. He slowly leaned his face toward mine until we were nose-to-nose. He kissed me slowly.

"That's a surprise," I noted.

"A happy surprise?" he asked.

"Very much so," I said.

And with that, we were inseparable, from Christmas to his graduation day. My parents, though supportive of our relationship, put rules in place so that we could respect their house while respecting our own boundaries as a young couple. There would be no "shacking up" in the Dailey household—so I moved to the basement. I visited Antonio at the dinner table and in the living room. At night, he went upstairs, I went downstairs, and we would chat on AOL Instant Messenger until we fell asleep.

Word got out at school about me and Antonio, and by Valentine's Day, the student body wondered what we would do. Public shows of love were a huge deal at Metro, but they weren't Antonio's style. I decided on a medium sized, black teddy bear with a box of chocolate candy. Antonio, on the other hand, surprised me with a bouquet of red roses; a bundle of balloons--one of which was a metallic rainbow balloon, representing gay pride; and a gift card for $50 to Maggiano's. He'd saved up a fortune in late 90s money from odd jobs.

That night, I told him I loved him. I said it first. I meant it. He said it back to me. Life was great for us.

We were a cute couple. Not sickening. Just cute. My mom and dad did a lot to make sure he felt loved and valued at home and I did my part everywhere else.

He ended up getting accepted to the University of Nebraska on a partial scholarship, with the balance paid for by a foundation my mom had discovered which gave scholarships to gay teenagers.

He would leave the day after graduation to begin a summer program in Lincoln for academic success. He'd earn some credits early and get into the swing of things on campus.

I liked him a lot, but I wasn't concerned about missing him. We'd both be busy doing the things we were supposed to do to have the lives we wanted.

We emailed each other often in those first weeks he was away, and we spoke on the phone about once a week. Those emails and calls dwindled throughout the summer as I got busier and busier with my own senior year, and presumably as Antonio began making new friends and going to class. He was usually upbeat when we did speak.

I didn't grow concerned until later that autumn, when he made the decision not to come home for Thanksgiving. He called my parents regularly and assured them he was okay, but the calls and emails to me eventually trickled to nothing at all.

Finally, on Christmas Eve, he came home. And what he told me changed everything.

When we were alone, I tried to kiss him, but he turned his head away from me.

"What's wrong?" I asked.

"Nothing's wrong, Eustace. Everything is right. Listen, I have something very important to tell you."

"What?"

"When I got to Lincoln, I was lonely and depressed. College was hard, man. Really hard. Even the summer class. But I found this great group of people to hang out with, and they took me to their church."

"Great! Did you like it?"

"I loved it. I fell in love with Jesus Christ and I haven't turned back since. I started going to Bible study and I began to learn that I wasn't happy because I wasn't living right. We're all born in sin and the only way to heaven is to confess our sins and give our lives over to Christ. And I did, Eustace. No more of that old sissy stuff we used to do. That's not of God. I was confused, trying to get back at my parents for giving up on me. But now I'm healed and I'm whole."

"Antonio, what?" I was so incredulous that I laughed.

"It's true, Eustace! I'm not gay anymore and you don't have to be, either!"

"It doesn't work that way. You can't just decide not to be gay anymore."

"I used to think that, too! But it takes willpower and prayer. If I can do it, you can do it."

The boy that I had loved had become a man that I didn't know.

"I think you'd better leave," I said.

"I'm already home, friend," he replied.

I looked around at my parent's living room.

"Then I'll leave."

"Eustace, I want you to experience the full love of the Lord like I have."

"One day you'll understand that I already experience His love. Everyday. Until then, goodnight. And goodbye."

I walked down the creaky stairs to my basement bedroom and buried my face into my pillow.

Antonio moved out soon after. Last I'd heard, he'd given up the scholarship he'd received from that foundation and found a job in Lincoln. Nobody I knew from Metro kept in contact with him.

"Hello, Antonio," I responded, eight years later in the airport baggage claim.

"It's been a long time," he said.

"Yes, it has. Well, goodbye."

I grabbed my bag and walked toward the exit.

"Eustace, wait." I turned around.

"Antonio, leave me alone."

"Please."

I stopped.

"If you're going to give me a *Watchtower* magazine, I'm not interested." He laughed.

"I'm not that guy anymore. I swear. Please. Let me give you a ride to your parents' house. I rented a car. I'm cheaper than a taxi. And a taxi driver won't have nearly as interesting a story to tell you. And I come with apologies. Eustace, please."

"I ain't walking to no parking lot. You pick me up out front like anybody else."

"Fair. I'll see you in ten minutes. Please, don't get in a cab. For real." I nodded.

God sure did have a terrible sense of humor. I might not have died on the plane, but I was surely in Hell already.

Antonio had a little more weight, a little more hair, and a little more charisma than I remembered. I hated seeing him again, but I did wonder what had happened to him.

"It's good seeing you man," he said as we pulled off.

"I wish I could say the same. But I'm willing to hear your story."

"Damn. I guess I deserve that."

"You guess? The last time I saw you, you were a Bible-thumping ex-gay that wanted me to be ex-gay with him."

"Yeah. I was that. But now I'm not."

"So what happened?"

"I realized that you were right all along. That you can't make somebody not be gay anymore. I was born this way—designed by God."

"Something tells me you didn't come to this realization overnight."

"Nah, not at all. You know I never liked learning anything the easy way. When I got to Lincoln, I got taken in by these nice people who happened to be part of a repressive church. Some might call it a cult. We weren't sacrificing animals or going on crime sprees, but they had all the hallmarks of a cult. We weren't allowed to question our leader, Pastor Mike. We needed to spend our entire weekends in service to the church. They considered it community service, but we were just out trying to recruit even more members. And we weren't supposed to socialize with anyone who wasn't in the church, unless we were recruiting for the church. That's why I didn't come home for Thanksgiving."

"But you came home for Christmas."

"Yes, for the last time. I told Pastor Mike that I could convince you to join our network. Maybe even come to Nebraska."

"But you always knew I wanted to go to the Northeast."

"Yes, I did. But that's how the church gets you. They had me convinced that I was going to Hell, man. That everything I knew was wrong. They convinced me that my depression was God's way of telling me that I was living in sin. I didn't need church. I needed a good therapist! I was still dealing with the trauma of getting kicked out of my parents home—and somehow still missing them. I missed your parents. And I missed you. I wasn't dealing with it at all and I latched onto the first wack jobs I could find."

"So that's how they got you. How did you get away?"

"I didn't. Not for another year. I did pretty poorly at Nebraska. Being in the church prevented me from adjusting into campus life. I didn't go to study groups. I didn't ask for help. I quit after the first year. I moved in with Pastor Mike and worked with his outdoors ministry. We went camping, read the Bible, prayed, sang songs. Petty corny, right?"

"Yeah, that's pretty bad."

"It gets worse. One night, Pastor Mike and I are chillin' by the fire. Everybody else is asleep. And he starts asking me if I ever get urges to go back to boys. And I say yeah. And he says he does, too. And he starts touching me on my shoulder and arms and says he can help me with those urges. And…he raped me, man."

"What?!"

"Yeah. He raped me. He covered my mouth, dragged me into the woods, away from the fire, and he penetrated me."

"Damn. I'm really sorry."

"Thanks. I was stunned. So stunned, I couldn't even think or speak. When we got back, I knew I had to leave. I was too ashamed to call the police or tell anybody, so I packed a bag and lived on the street for a few days. When I ran out of money, I went back to campus to the only place I thought I could get help: The Jackie Gaughan Multicultural Center. It was the only place on campus where I knew for sure I could find a black person.

"When I did find that person, my whole life changed. I got emergency housing. I got the counseling I needed. I found a good church to attend. And when I got my grades up, they were gracious about letting me transfer to another school. Everybody knew it would be best for me to get a new start someplace else. So I ended up in Chicago. I graduated from Chicago State two years ago."

"Wow. What do you do now?"

"I work for a nonprofit organization that fights religious oppression of gay people. I work with a team that counsels LGBT youth who have been abused by churches. I'm hoping to get my Masters in Social Work some day."

"So you're a good guy, now."

"I been a bad guy long enough, don't you think?"

I sat in silence while I let his words sink in.

"Eustace, this is a long time coming. I didn't reach out to you sooner because I honestly thought you'd never want to hear from me again. But I'm sorry. I treated you terribly when I was in that cult and you didn't deserve it. You always treated me like a king. So did your parents. I was at a very low point in my life, and I should have been man enough to see how my beliefs were damaging me and everybody I cared about. I hope you can accept my apology and see that the life I live now is a lot better than the one I was living."

"I don't think anybody has ever apologized to me and meant it as sincerely as you," I said.

"You either have really shitty friends or really good friends," he joked.

"Good, mostly. Look, I'm sorry about what happened to you. If I'd known more about how these religious groups operate, I might have had better advice for how to leave one."

"You were only 17. I was 18. How were we supposed to know what to do? This wasn't your fault by a longshot. You always wanted to have the answers."

"Wanted to. And now it seems like I've got nothing but more questions."

"You look like you've been through some things yourself."

I paused and looked at him.

"Nothing like what you've been through. For what it's worth, I'm just a boring management consultant with a side gig as a photographer."

"You have never been boring."

"I am now, man. When you're around the guys I'm around, you realize how insignificant you really are."

"Who *are* you? Boring? Insignificant? Did Harvard treat you that badly?"

"No. Not at all. I had a blast. I'm just not...I'm just not sure what's next."

"Neither was I. I guess we never really know what's next. Hey, look at that. You're almost home."

"Yeah. Almost."

"You think your parents would want to hear from me?"

"I think they'd like that a lot."

"Then I'll call them. After Thanksgiving."

"Where are you spending the holiday?"

"With my mother and father. They finally came around. And my boyfriend. We've come a long way."

"I see. How long have you been in a relationship?"

"About three years now. Found me a good dude at Chicago State. Reminds me a lot of you. Always keeps me on my toes."

"That's good, Antonio. I'm glad you stopped me in the airport."

"Me too. I hope we can stay in touch." I smiled and nodded at him.

"Let me help you with your bag," he offered.

"I'm good. Really. Thank you, though."

"Okay. Be well, Eustace."

"Same to you, Antonio."

I shut the car door and waved goodbye to Antonio. I turned around to face my childhood home and the next three days of my life. I walked up the stairs and knocked on the door.

"Hey baby," my mom said.

"Hey mama." I dropped my bag to the floor and hugged her.

"What's all this for?" she asked.

"It's been a long...it's just been a long time."

She held me tightly. I was relieved to be back in a place where people knew me, loved me, and didn't know what I had become over the past few months.

The National Mall is the best site that a Washington traveler could see when headed back home by air. When you're sitting in that plane and it sharply dips, you think you're about to die. But then you see the monuments and the Capitol as the aircraft levels out. You know then that you're home and the plane will be touching down in moments.

And life goes on.

Dear Eustace,

Congratulations! The University of New Mexico is pleased to welcome you to our Master of Fine Arts Program in Photography.

We enjoyed reviewing your portfolio and your personal statement. We feel that you will be a fine addition to our program.

Additionally, we would like to offer you a Regent's Fellowship. This fellowship covers the full cost of tuition, room, and board for the entirety of your time at UNM, so long as you maintain high academic standards and perform artistic service to the community surrounding the university.

Eustace, you should know that we are ready to welcome you for the term beginning in January. We know this is a very quick turnaround, but we feel strongly about you joining this family of artists and would like to see you as soon as possible.

Please let us know your decision.

Sincerely,
Dr. Jayne Hedlund
Director of Admissions of the College of Fine Arts

Dear Adrian,

Please see below…biiiiiiiitch!!!!!!! What I'ma do??????

Y.I.T.B.,
Eustace

Dear Eustace,

Biiiiiiiiiitch! OMG! Congratulations!
You better go get that free degree!!!

Y.I.T.B.,
Adrian

Dear Adrian,

I'm scared shitless.

Y.I.T.B,
Eustace

Dear Eustace,

Man the fuck up.

Y.I.T.B.,
Adrian

Dear Julian,

I've been a terrible friend lately. I've had a lot going on in my life the past few weeks. But I think I'm on the verge of a breakthrough.

I've just been offered a full ride to a photography program at the University of New Mexico! But I don't know if I should take it.

I've made a good life for myself in DC. I am surrounded by good friends and a really good job. And I do pretty well at photography on my own, without formal training. Most photographers learn on their own, right?

But this opportunity…I could really go from good to great. And even though I love DC, I think the time away would be good for me.

I don't know what to do. Any advice?

Regards,
Eustace.

Dear Eustace Dailey,

Wow. First of all, congratulations! UNM will be lucky to have you, if you go.

You have quite a decision to make. I don't know what I would do if I were you. When I finished college, I decided that was enough for me. I knew my audience better than any stodgy old faculty would. And I knew there was nothing more I could be taught about music. I needed to put in the work on the ground, not in a classroom. And I needed to do it while I was still young and pretty.

But you...I don't know. Maybe a classroom would be good for you. Maybe being away from DC is what you need. You've already moved halfway across the country once, when you left the Midwest to come to college. Who's to say you can't do it again?

You're single, right? No kids? Not even a pet? Nothing is holding you in DC.

Your real friends will support you and understand if you leave, and they'll know you're only a phone call or an email away.

I can't tell you if this is the right grad program for you. I can't tell you if you'd love New Mexico.

But I know one thing for certain: bomb ass photographers need to see the world.

Only you can decide if New Mexico is the right place. Only you know if now is the right time.

One love.
Julian

Chapter Seven:
December 2005

My parents said go.
    Adrian said go.
    Julian said go.
My heart said stay.
My brain said go.
That's a majority.

Friends and family, this may come as a shock to most of you, but earlier this year, I applied to one of the best graduate programs in photography that I could find. I got in! Two years from now, God-willing, you will be looking at a photographer with an MFA from the University of New Mexico. Thank you all for believing in my craft. I'll be starting in January, so all my DC folks, meet me for one last drink!

My Facebook page flooded with congratulatory notes and expressions of surprise from friends, family, and Frat. I could hardly believe it myself.

A loud knock interrupted the peacefulness of my evening a few hours later. I looked through the peephole and saw JJ standing there. I took a deep breath and turned the knob.

"Hey," I said.

"Hey."

"What's up?"

"You gonna let me in?"

I pushed the door open the rest of the way and allowed JJ entry.

"I guess you heard the news," I said.

"Grad school, huh?"

"Yeah. Grad school."

"When did you apply?"

"This summer. On a whim. I applied to one place."

"And that place had to be New Mexico?"

"I didn't even think I'd get in."

"But you applied. You know, in fifteen minutes after I read your bullshit ass Facebook post, I researched ten MFA programs in Photography that you could have applied to that are within 15 miles of an Amtrak station in the Northeast."

"JJ, please don't do this."

He walked past me and into the middle of my living room. He looked around with his hands in his leather jacket.

"Why the fuck do you want to go all the way to New Mexico?"

"Their program is really good. Top five in the nation."

"They got camera school over here, Eustace!"

"Camera school?" I laughed.

"Don't you even think about laughing at me. The fuck do you think you're doing here?"

"Not this." I walked away from him and he grabbed my arm.

"Get off me," I shook him loose and he backed up.

"You have it made, nigga. You don't have a care in the world. Partying every weekend. Stacking checks. They got that where you going?"

"I have a chance to do something I love."

"Photography? You already do that—and you do it well. And you get paid for it!"

"But I could be better. I could be like a real artist. And the life I'm living? Who cares! If I am gonna party every weekend, I can party anywhere. You think they don't party in New Mexico?"

"That's not the fucking point."

"Then you tell me the fucking point."

"The fucking point is that you're leaving me when I need you the most." I stared at him for a long time and tilted my head to the side.

"I'm starting to think you are literally insane. What are you talking about? You don't *need* me."

"Yes, I do! You're my best friend."

"No, we're not. We are not best friends, JJ. We were lovers. We might have been friends, once. We might have even been best friends. But we crossed the line. And when we crossed that line, we lost ourselves." JJ's eyes narrowed.

"That's the dumbest shit I ever heard!"

"Oh, come on, JJ!"

"This is killing me, Eustace! Don't you know I can't do none of this without you?"

"None of what? You are almost done with law school. I wasn't with you studying. I wasn't practicing moot court with you. That was you."

"But the moral support, man."

"This isn't about moral support. You know it. Please don't be like this."

"You didn't even tell me you were applying to schools! Why would you hide that from me?"

"I didn't tell anyone."

"I don't care about anybody else. I'm talking about you and me."

"I...I don't know. I just did it. I wanted something different for myself. And now the opportunity is here and I'm taking it."

"When did you apply?"

"This summer."

"When this summer?"

"I don't know."

"Don't lie to me!"

"It was around my birthday."

"Oh. I see what this is now."

"Do you?"

"Oh yes!" He nodded his head vigorously. "You made this irrational decision after I told you I planned to propose to Sylvia."

"Are you fucking kidding me? Are you so arrogant that you can't see me making a decision without you in mind?"

"You never could handle what I have with her."

"JJ, get out of my house."

"No. Not until you admit that this whole thing is a childish reaction to me trying to live my life. You know we can't be what you want us to be."

"Who the fuck do you think you are?!" I walked to JJ and got right in his face.

"Jeremy Jacob Carter! And I am tired of your shit."

"And I am goddamned tired of yours! You can't have us both, asshole! You made your choice. You chose Sylvia. I got the message loud and clear."

"And what message was that?"

"That you will never be ready for me to love you."

"Oh, you think?"

"I know. And you know something else?"

"What?"

"No matter who you marry...no matter how much time passes...I can have you whenever I want to." I punctuated each phrase with a point to his chest.

"Oh, it's like that?" he asked.

"That's the way it is. And that's the way it will always be. You want it all. That's why you're marrying Sylvia. That's why you want to be a lawyer. You want the house with the picket fence and the two and a half children. You want this buppie American dream at any cost. And it burns you up that I can be as free as I want to be. That I can give it all up—including you—and still be happy. You hate that."

"That's not true."

"Isn't it, though? You want it all, plus me. You want me to always be in the wings, pining after you, wanting you, loving you. But I'm not part of your new little family, JJ. You gave her a ring."

"I gave you a ring, too, fool!" He snatched my hand and put it in my face.

"You gave me a fucking fraternity ring, big fucking deal. You can have the shit back."

"Fuck you, Eustace. Keep the damn ring. Hock it when you get to New Mexico for all I fucking care. I'm outta here." He stormed past me and walked toward the door. I walked right behind him. As he turned the knob, I placed my hand on the door and held it closed.

"Back up off me, dude," he said, struggling with the door. It gave way a little, but I closed it and swatted his hand away. I locked it again and put the chain on.

"Let me go," he said. His back stiffened and he refused to face me.

"No." I wrapped my arms around him and hugged him from behind.

"Just let me go," he whispered.

"I can't do that," I whispered back. I kissed his ear. He shivered and held me back.

"You remember the first time we met?" he asked me through chattering teeth.

"Of course I do," I whispered. "Spring 2001, the night I crossed. I saw you across the room with the rest of the Bros from Alpha Chapter. I always felt like you guys had 'the look,' you know?

Like what a Beta man was supposed to be. But you...you even more than the rest."

He leaned his head back until my lips brushed his ear. I continued.

"You were the center of gravity. So handsome. Confident. Everything the process took from me, you had. I wanted to know you so bad. I'd seen you around the city countless times, and you know what? I silently wished I could be your friend. I never in my wildest dreams thought all this would have happened between us."

His voice trembling, he spoke: "I felt the same way."

"You never told me that."

"Confidence. Too much of it can destroy any semblance of humility. I noticed you the moment you started attending fraternity events. I started coming to your chapter events just to see you. Everything you were, I wanted to be. Every little thing you did to assert your pride, I noticed, down to the rainbow socks."

"I was afraid to introduce myself to you."

"So was I. But you know, we didn't first meet the night you crossed. I..."

He turned around and hugged me at the waist.

"I was obsessed with you. With making sure that you made it. When Beta Chapter felt your line was ready to be seen, I was there. Any time you were blindfolded, I was there. In the darkness, there are those Brothers who want to abuse and mistreat pledges—I have been that guy. In the darkness, there are also those Brothers who help you, who guide you, who hold your hand, who whisper those words of power that help you through."

"That was you?"

"Almost every time."

"Why didn't you tell me?"

"I didn't want to scare you. I was scaring myself. I didn't know what was happening to me. I still don't know."

I closed my eyes and kissed the side of his head slowly, caressing his face. I kissed him all over, from his forehead to his eyelids to his cheeks to his chin. I didn't stop to look at him. If I stopped, it would become real. I just took the moment where it was, as it was.

My lips found their way to his lips as his hands found their way to my face. I kissed him and it was everything I wanted. I loved him with everything I had and the only way I could show him was in this kiss.

Pressure.

Passion.

Love.

His mouth opened for me and our tongues met. His hands slid from my cheeks to my ears to the back of my head, pulling me even closer to him until our noses pressed. I tilted my head to the side and lowered my jaw so that I could taste more of him. Our tongues danced and twisted and tangled, clicking and smacking so loudly that I was certain my whole floor could hear us.

I slid my arms around him, underneath his jacket, and held him close to me. Our chests pressed together and I felt his heart thumping against mine. I pulled him away from me long enough to take his jacket off and toss it onto the sofa.

"Look at me," he said. I stared at his chest as it quickly rose and fell.

"Up here," he directed. I looked into his face.

"I'm sorry. For everything I've ever put you through."

I nodded.

"And you're right," he continued.

"About what?"

"You can have me whenever you want."

He looked up at me with his big brown eyes.

"Promise?" I asked. I grabbed him softly by his neck and pushed him back against the door while I kissed him again. With my free hand, I explored his body, quickly finding my way under his black turtleneck shirt. He shivered again. His hands wandered all over my torso, from top to bottom.

We walked to my bedroom. He picked me up, kissed me, and laid me on my bed. He climbed on top of me and continued kissing me, holding my hands over my head.

He sighed. I opened my eyes.

"I love you," I said. He opened his eyes and gazed into mine.

"I love you," he echoed.

"...and because I love you, we have to stop."

He froze, stared at me, and rolled over.

"So...you really still leaving?"

"Yes...I am. I have to." He took me by the hand.

"I want you to have a good life, Eustace. I really do. I know this...all this...is just for right now. But I love you. And I'd do anything for you." I turned to look at him in the eyes.

"Would you let me go?" He looked back at me.

"Is that what you want?"

"It's what I need."

"Then yeah. I'll let you go, Eustace."

He hugged me tightly and nuzzled my neck.

"I'll never forget you," he whispered.

"I'm not dying, you know." He smiled and his teeth grazed my neck.

"I know. But I won't see you for a while. And I guess it's best that way."

"If I didn't already know the answer, I'd tell you that you could just...you know...come with me." His grip on my hand tightened.

"...but I already know. You're not going to give up your life for me. And I'm not going to give up my life for you. It's not like that for either of us. So I guess...it is what it is."

"I wish things could be different, Eustace."

"Yeah. Sure you do. But we'll always have tonight, right?"

"Yeah. Tonight."

For the last time, JJ fell asleep in my arms. When I woke up the next morning, he was already gone. A few days later, I was gone, too.

Part Three:
Barbados
Spring Break 2016

Beta Chi Phi Fraternity, Inc.

ΒΧΦ

From the Desk of Adrian Collins
National Executive Director

Dear Brothers,

It's been far too long since we've seen one another. Before my schedule becomes impossible to plan around, due to the upcoming National Convention, I'm hoping that you will join me as a guest in Barbados for a brotherly retreat at a villa on Mullins Bay.

Your children are welcome.

Yours in the bond,
Brother Adrian

Chapter One:
Adrian

"And then we literally drove off into the sunset. Destination Brooklyn."

Zion sat on the white leather chaise near me and his dad's bed, where Isaiah and I reclined in our pajamas. Isaiah's tablet rested in his lap and he grinned throughout the retelling of our love story, which was also the story of how Zion was born. My laptop was off to the side, idling but ready for me to resume work on our family foundation.

"Wait. You mean after all that, you two literally rode off into the sunset?"

"Yeah. That's exactly how it happened," Isaiah said. Zion's serious face melted into a fit of loud, obnoxious laughter.

"You guys! That's so gay!" He clutched his chest and laughed even harder.

"What?" Isaiah asked.

"That's how it happened!" I said.

"You guys. That is literally the most sickeningly romantic story I've ever heard. Like literally, it's like Romeo & Romeo, but black as hell. And gay."

"You have gay parents, fool. How else was it supposed to be?" Isaiah asked.

"I dunno, dad. I guess I was expecting something else."

"Regardless. When you came into this world, you were surrounded in love. Your dad, your mom, and me. I don't know how we got through those first few years, but we did it," I said.

"Papa?" Zion asked.

"Yeah?"

"Did my mom…did she hate you?" I looked down.

"We weren't the best of friends after she found out about me and your dad."

"But they made it work that first year," Isaiah said.

"How did you feel when she died?" Zion asked.

"What's with all the questions today?" Isaiah asked. Zion shrugged.

"I dunno. I don't remember my mom. I guess she's been on my mind lately."

"We were all devastated when your mom died. But we were grateful that you were safe."

"You miss her, huh?" Isaiah asked. Zion nodded.

"Yeah. I do. Not in the way that you miss somebody you know and loved. But like...in the way that you see what everybody else has and wonder what it feels like. I mean, I love y'all both. It's not about having two fathers. It's more about...seeing other kids at school with their moms, having that relationship."

"I know it's tough. And we've tried to make sure Grandma Liz and Grandma Gloria are in your life as much as possible. But nothing can take the place of a mom," I said.

"I wish...I wish Taina had made it. Gotten the help she needed while she was alive. But I know she's looking down on you from heaven. She must be so proud of the man you're becoming. Just like we are," Isaiah added.

Zion smiled.

"Thanks, Dad. Thanks, Papa." He rose from the chaise and walked over to Isaiah. He hugged him, and Isaiah kissed him on the forehead. He walked to my side of the bed and hugged me. I held him.

"You're the best son I could have asked for," I whispered to him, stifling the tears.

"I love you, Papa. Goodnight." He shuffled away barefoot on our white carpet and closed the door behind him. I wiped away a single tear from my eye.

"Whew. That never gets easier, does it?" Isaiah asked. He kissed me on the cheek.

"Never. We've always been super honest with him, and he's always been transparent with us. Still, I can't imagine how hard it must be to deal with having gay parents and a dead mother."

Isaiah chuckled.

"What?" I questioned.

"No matter how hard it is, he'll always be rich," he laughed. I smirked.

"No. *You're* rich. He's a rich man's son."

"He's had all the advantages I didn't. He'll be fine."

"I hope so," I sighed. I rose from the bed to close the blinds of our Baltimore condominium overlooking the inner harbor.

"Did you tell him about Barbados yet?" he asked.

"No. I'm going to talk to him about it in the morning, though."

"He's going to be so excited. Too bad you keep planning your little excursions when basketball season is in full swing."

"We have our time, you know that."

"I know we do. I just feel like I've missed so many fun times. And I miss your friends, too. I like them a lot."

"They like you, too."

"Calen coming with y'all?"

"Nah, no line brothers on this trip. They're all coming to convention, though. As they should."

"Yeah, your first one as National Executive Director. Talk about full circle, huh?"

"Seems like just yesterday I pledged. But yeah, this group is going to be small. If everybody shows up, it will be me and Zion, JJ and Three Jay, Ian, Miles, and Eustace."

"Wait. You finna have Eustace and JJ on the same island?"

"Yeah."

"You think that's a good idea?"

"Oh please, they're ancient history."

"JJ is Eustace's kryptonite."

"Eustace been off JJ. He's had plenty of boyfriends since then."

"Yeah. Okay. 'Boyfriends.'"

"Well it's too late to do anything about it now, the invitations are already out."

"I'm glad production won't be there."

"Oh God, never. I don't mind the cameras being around when it's just me and the athlete's wives, but I would never put my actual friends on screen."

"Although…"

"Isaiah, don't even start."

"I'm just saying! Bravo would pay big bucks for a spin-off to *High Heels and Basketball!*"

"We don't need big bucks. My boys are successful enough."

"You can never be too successful."

"We really gonna do this tonight?"

Isaiah smiled.

"I love you, Mr. Collins."

"I love you, too, Mr. Aiken."

Chapter Two:
Miles

Although I hadn't had dreadlocks in many years, when I cruised Sunset Boulevard with my top down, I imagined my long-gone locs whipping in the wind.

The sun baked Los Angeles, as it did most days. I listened to my favorite pop station on the way to work every morning. When I heard the first chords of the organ on my latest jam, I turned the volume up and sang along.

"You used to call me on my cellll phoooooone!" I crooned.

"Oh God," my wife said.

"What?" I asked.

"Is this song not played out yet?"

"Nope! I know when that hotline bling!"

"Thank God you're fine. Singing is not your ministry."

"I love you, too," I said.

Not a day went by that I didn't feel like the luckiest man alive. I had two great jobs and an awesome wife who was smarter than me. I told people she was a spy for the government. She was actually a mathematician—the Associate Director for the Center for Encrypted Functionalities at UCLA. There weren't too many black female mathematicians with positions like hers.

As for my jobs, I became the librarian I always wanted to be. Specifically, I served as the Arts Librarian at UCLA. I managed a whole division devoted to art history, film, television, and everything cool about pop culture. The job kept me busy, but my bosses were quite understanding of my other work as a model.

It was L.A., after all.

Shortly after Eustace's huge art show in 2005, my career path mirrored his. I got calls for local and regional fashion shows nonstop. I got a few print ads in local publications, too. By the time I got my MLS degree, I had to make some tough choices—did I want to be a librarian or did I want to be a model? New York called.

I decided that I didn't have to choose. I answered New York's call and joined one of the most notable talent management companies in the world. I also took a job at the circulation desk of a neighborhood library.

I joined the New York Alumni Chapter of Beta Chi Phi and attended meetings faithfully, too.

My agency connected me to awesome photographers and helped me develop my portfolio. I gained more print work as well as more runway work.

The agency also tried to send me on auditions for television shows and films, but in those days I refused to even go. Moving images weren't my thing. Still photography and walking a runway were more my speed.

Even though I enjoyed the fruits of consistent modeling work and a regular paycheck with benefits from the New York Public Library, my biggest break came in 2009, a few years after I moved to the Big Apple.

Every now and then, I facilitated the toddler story time at Jefferson Market Library, a castle-like building in the West Village. About ten to twelve kids usually attended, mostly with their nannies. This one time, though, a black woman that appeared to be about my age was there with her young daughter. I chose the book *Nappy Hair* by Carolivia Herron for the occasion. As I read the book, I noticed the woman filming me with her phone. I didn't mind—I was used to being recognized from my print ads.

The following week, there were about ten more families at the story hour for the toddlers. Most of them were black women. All had their camera phones out. I found it interesting, but I didn't think much of it.

By the third week, there were about a hundred women there, black, white, Latina, you name it. They clapped when I came out to read the latest book, *Please, Baby, Please* by Spike Lee and Tonya Lewis Lee.

I was confused, yet happy to see so many more people of color at the library. I asked no questions that week.

But the fourth week, when the crowd doubled to two hundred people, leaving the children with barely enough room to sit, I had to ask the question.

"Ladies...and gentlemen...welcome to the Jefferson Market Library. But I gotta ask...what brings you here today?"

"You!" the crowd said in unison as they clapped and cheered!

I pointed to the book in my hand, *Honey, I Love* by Eloise Greenfield.

"Y'all know I'm not the author, right?"

The crowd laughed.

"You know you're #LibraryBoo, right?" a mom asked.

"Library…boo? Like a ghost?" She laughed.

"No, like boo! Like babe, handsome man, hunk! You're a viral celebrity!"

"What the…"

She came to the front of the room and showed me her phone.

"Listen, just Google #LibraryBoo and see what comes up," she instructed. I did as she said and discovered pages upon pages of short articles about me, along with pictures of me in my various outfits. The most notable was my brown, tweed, three-piece suit and red bowtie ensemble from a month ago. It was a slim-fitting number that happened to accentuate my bicep, thighs, and butt.

"Oh," I said. I did my job and wore nice clothes. I wasn't sure what the fuss was all about personally.

I could tell from her facial expression that the lady who took the time to show me her articles didn't appreciate my lack of a response. Living with my Asperger's Syndrome was an ongoing fight. I was wired differently from most people and interpreting social cues was one of my main challenges. I didn't necessarily feel differently than other people, but I knew I had to do a little more to make sure I wasn't misunderstood.

"I'm sorry," I began gingerly. "I appreciate you sharing these articles with me. I would have never known about it otherwise. Thank you."

I smiled. The lady smiled back.

After about two months of growing crowds, New York Public Library took note of my work. They expanded story hour and hired additional "librarians" for assistance. They were part time models who had an Afro-Latino look about them and were fluent enough in English to read children's books aloud. I trained them in all they needed to know.

Then I got promoted. For the first time, my life as a model intersected with my life as a Librarian. With the director of communications for NYPL, I developed the Sexy Readers, Sexy Books campaign. For six months, my face was on billboards, newspaper and magazine ads, and on commercials for the library. I visited book clubs for local branches, hosted sip & read events, and even hosted a few fundraisers.

That's how I met my wife, the good Doctor Carly Sawyer. I found this statuesque, dreadlocked goddess hovering by the punchbowl while her colleagues were engaged in a conversation with one another. I could tell by her raised eyebrows and quick glances that she was listening, but wasn't interested.

"Hi," I said.

"Hello," she said softly.

"My name is Miles. Thank you for coming."

"Carly Sawyer." We shook hands.

"Are you enjoying yourself?" I asked.

"Enjoyment is relative, isn't it?"

"Let's go for a walk. You look like you could use the break?" She smiled as I gave her my arm and we walked toward the terrace.

I found out she was a brilliant professor of mathematics at NYU and the rest was history.

We dated for three months before I proposed. We were married six months after that.

I like what I like when I like it.

Our career paths took us to UCLA as a package deal when she joined her super-spy, code cracking institute. By that time, she convinced me to try some acting gigs as they became available. I got a new agent and started booking small roles on sitcoms, and later dramas.

However, I remained loyal to being a librarian, and I refused any gigs that didn't work with my schedule. Although, truthfully, UCLA had no qualms with as many appearances as I could muster. The combination of a brilliant black mathematician on their faculty and the black supermodel librarian made for many interesting articles in campus publications.

"I hope you enjoy Barbados," she told me in her expressionless voice.

"I think I will."

"Make sure Eustace brings his camera."

"He always does these days."

"Good."

"Wish you could come!"

"I wasn't invited. This is clearly a boys' trip."

"Are you disappointed?"

"No. We're backpacking this summer."

"True."

I loved having a wife on the spectrum. To a casual observer, we were detached from one another. But to me, our quick, even terse conversations were markers of a deep emotional relationship. We were hyper-focused on our goals and didn't give a fuck about what others thought of our relationship.

My life was damn good and I couldn't wait to tell my Brothers about it in person.

Chapter Three:
Eustace

"You really think anybody is gonna buy this thing?" I asked my agent.

"*Eustace Dailey: The Early Years*? Are you kidding me? This thing is gonna sell like hotcakes, kid."

"I dunno." I cradled the galley. Mary Carlisle, who had had enough of my shit, snatched it away from me.

"Well let's shelve the damn thing, then."

"Okay, Mary, damn! You know how I am."

"Let the doubts stay in the past, my friend. I wouldn't take you on as a client if I didn't think you were a damn good photographer."

"Thank you, Mary. I appreciate having you in charge of this part of my career. I just take pictures, you know? I never thought much about publishing a book."

"Well here you are, kid. Hopefully one of many. Now you know you've got to work hard at promoting yourself. The publisher is gonna get it on the shelves, but it's up to you to get the buyers there. You gonna hire a PR person?"

"I guess so."

"The clock is ticking. Think about it, but not too long. You've got deep networks—use them!"

"Thanks Mary. I appreciate you."

"Ditto."

Me and self-doubt were best friends at the least opportune times. After two years of formal education and nine years of full-time professional photography, one would think that I'd have no problem publishing my first book. *Eustace Dailey: The Early Years* was to highlight the first five years of my career, from my breakthrough portrait with Miles, to my Parisian street series. Viewed together, these photos represented the body of work which earned me a MacArthur genius grant a few years ago.

Yeah…I got that. It was dope.

Even with all the accolades and awards, my self-doubt lingered. I pushed through most days, was pulled through others, and rarely—very rarely—I was incapacitated by it. But usually, I pushed through.

I had some decisions to make about my book, though. Whether I was personally ready or not, the book was ready and had a Fall 2016 release date. I had time, but not enough for my liking. I had about six months to either hire a PR team or figure out how to do it myself.

The choices I had to make for myself now were surreal. I had a real book coming out. I had a real full-time career as a photographer. I had real clients, real fans, and real money in the bank. Thankfully, the money I had socked away during my days as a consultant kept me afloat right after I completed my MFA. I had finished school in the middle of the financial crisis of 2007-08 and immediately came to New York, where jobs were scarce, and nobody wanted to pay for photography. Between my savings and a part time gig teaching photography as an elective at a posh independent school in Midtown, I had little to worry about. The economy eventually rebounded, and I had steady clients and widening networks.

The MacArthur was a surprise a few years ago. I guess I hob-knobbed with the right folks during my early career and they recognized me with a grant that allowed me to move into an artist's apartment building in Brooklyn that came with dedicated studio space. It was my haven and my cure for whatever ailed me. I loved working, but I cherished being at home.

I arrived at the apartment shortly after my talk with my agent and checked my mailbox. It was stuffed with junk mail, catalogs, and a few envelopes. Two were on stationary from the fraternity. One was addressed to me, and the other to Ian Kenney. I opened mine on the spot, read it, and smiled.

"Barbados! I'm in that thing."

I bounded up the two flights of stairs and unlocked my apartment door. Ian Kenney, all six feet and four inches of him, was sprawled out on my black leather sofa watching the latest episode of *High Heels and Basketball.*

"Hey," I said with a smile.

"What up? Whatchu grinning about?" He smiled back.

"You'll never guess where we're about to go."

Chapter Four:
Ian

Words really can't express how much I love Eustace Dailey.

I know people say that all the time--"Words can't express…"—then they go on to use a bunch of words that do exactly that. But for me, I honestly can't come up with the right words. Instead, here's how I got here, on Eustace's couch with an invitation to Barbados in my hands.

I became a Brother of Beta Chi Phi Fraternity, Incorporated, at Pi Chapter, Morehouse College in Atlanta, Georgia, in the Spring of 2014. I was number 11 of 11—the tail of the line.

Making line for Beta was one of the best days of my life. Pi Chapter had lines in alternating years, so my junior year was my first chance to even try. As soon as you step foot on campus, you find out that "discretion is key." You weren't supposed to tell anyone about your interest in a fraternity. You were supposed to show your interest by attending events regularly and by getting to know the members.

Unfortunately, getting to know the members was a bigger challenge than I expected. The chapter wasn't doing a lot of community service or public programs. On the rare occasion that I shared a class with a member, they'd run off quickly, leaving me no opportunity to get to know them. Every now and then I'd corner a member, but they ignored me or changed the subject entirely.

Luckily, I was one confident and persistent motherfucker.

I did my research everywhere that I could, from the campus library to message boards on the internet. I memorized previous lines of the chapter, poems I'd heard were important to Betas, and the Greek alphabet. I needed to be thorough if I wanted to join the dopest boys on the yard.

I kept my grades up, even as a Chemistry major, one of the most rigorous courses of study at Morehouse. More than becoming a Beta, I wanted to be a pharmacist, so graduating at—or near—the top of my class was important. But having excellent grades wouldn't hurt my quest to Greekdom. Since the Betas weren't that interested in getting to know me, I'd have to have the perfect application when the time came.

In spite of it all, I nearly missed rush. No matter how much preparation you have in terms of knowledge and key facts, if you don't have a relationship with the members, you're never going to get in.

Unless you happen to see the rush flyer, as I did. One tradition that I never knew, until it was almost too late, was that Pi Chapter posted a single flier in advance of rush, always in Dansby Hall, always in the Mathematics Department, and always on a single gold sheet of paper. Only one flier was ever necessary—there was never more than one.

That's not how rush was supposed to be advertised, according to all the literature I had downloaded online over the years, but that's the way Pi Chapter did it and I'd have to deal.

When I happened by the flyer, I saw that rush would be the next day. I had a minor panic attack, but the moment had been prepared for. My black suit hung in my closet, already dry-cleaned and pressed, waiting for this day.

With a fresh haircut and a portfolio filled with copies of my resume, in case I needed them, I entered our campus chapel and was dismayed to see at least 60 other young men there, looking as sharp and polished as I felt. I had never known Beta to have large lines on this campus and I knew I'd have to be twice as good as everyone else to even get a second look.

After rush, I completed my application, turned it in on time, and waited. Within a few weeks, I received word that I had made it! Remembering that discretion was key, I told my mom and dad and no one else. I didn't even tell my roommate or best friends on campus. I disappeared into the background as the process moved forward.

In about five weeks, we were done. We had about another week to practice for our probate—more accurately a new member presentation, but only old people called them that.

During the practice for our probate, we were finally given our line names:

1. Slip-N-Slide
2. Chosen Legacy
3. The Heretic
4. The Heir Up There
5. Involuntary Manslaughter
6. True Religion
7. Luck of the Draw
8. Sanctioned Tradition
9. Affirmative

10. The People's Choice

11. Skintight

Our collective name was "The Inheritance of a Perfect Tradition" also known as "What Are the Odds?"

At first, I was excited to even have a line name. The Brothers had been so mean to us throughout the process, it seemed like we might never even get the privilege. But things weren't adding up, from the day we got our names to the day of our show.

We marched out to the massive cheers of the public. Yet, as we marched, hand to shoulder of the line brother in front of us, the energy was off. Our prophytes barely spoke as we marched, as though they didn't want to be there. No Brothers preened over us and none whispered affirmations in our ears as we trudged forward to the location of our show.

We arrived at Kilgore to a waiting crowd. We performed our greetings, and then we stepped. In each formation during our performance, half of our line brothers were always in the front—the even numbers. I hadn't noticed it before, but things came together as we went through the show.

When we introduced ourselves, half of our line brothers always got cheers and fraternity calls from the chapter—the even numbers.

When it ended, about half of us received gifts from the chapter, aside from our line jackets—the even numbers.

And when we did receive our line jackets, the even numbers got white jackets and the odds got black jackets.

It was right in front of our faces the whole time: The even numbers were "The Inheritance of a Perfect Tradition." "What are the Odds?" was not the name of a line—it was a statement about the rest of us.

Soon after our probate, I called a secret meeting with my line brothers who also failed to gain the chapter's favor.

"Bruhs, I'm not imagining this, am I?" I asked.

"No, you're not," my Number 3 said.

"They been treating us different since the very beginning," Number 7 said.

"But why? Why did they pick us if they didn't want us?"

"You already know why, LB.   Beta's process is mostly quantitative, and incidentally qualitative.   We're here because we got more points than the rest, and because the grad chapter in charge followed the rules," Number 5 said.

"It's clear. They only wanted five of us, but they had to take six more because we had the grades, the community service, the recommendations—we *are* the line," said Number 9.

"You notice what the other half is like?" Number 7 asked.

"I can't lie. They're not like us," I said.

"They wild," Number 7 said.

"Not very…God, I hate to say it…polished." Number 5 said.

"They don't act like how Betas I know back home act," Number 1 contributed. "They're not refined, super into themselves, and never really gave a fuck about the rest of us. And to see that they're the ones that the chapter favors fucking grinds my gears. We did the work. We lifted them up during this process. We made sure the tests got passed, even when we knew those guys hadn't even studied."

"It's like they knew they would pass anyway," I said.

"Other chapters have this problem," Number 3 began. "But the way my cousin tells me, the public is not even supposed to know there is a division."

"Our line jackets don't even match," I said.

"Ain't that some shit?" my Number 9 said.

"So what do we do?" asked Number 3.

"Let's play it by ear," I suggested. "We have a month left in school. Maybe things will get better."

But things didn't get better. The more the brothers in the outer circle tried to do things in and for the chapter, like community service and programs, the less respect members of the inner circle had to give us. They wanted to be on center stage—God forbid anybody with an odd number did any work in Beta's name.

The national convention was in Memphis, Tennessee that summer. The inner circle, of course, was paid for. The outer circle had to make a dollar out of fifteen cents. I turned out being the only ostracized Brother who was able to attend the convention. I knew that I had to learn as much about Beta as possible if I was going to fix the chapter.

My line brothers were in Memphis to party, so I didn't see a lot of them at all. When I did see them, they sneered and ignored me.

One convention agenda item included the Generations panel: Brothers who were celebrating five-year crossing anniversaries, from 2009 all the way back to 1974. The two-hour panel was an excellent opportunity to gain perspective on the changes the fraternity had undergone since its founding.

Representing the 15th anniversary Brothers from the Spring of 1999 were Adrian Collins, the Sigma Chapter initiate who led the Aiken Family Foundation; and corporate litigator Jeremy Jacob Carter from Alpha Chapter. They had been friends for over a decade, ever since they served on the board together, Adrian as National Second Vice President, and JJ as National Undergraduate Member at Large.

I listened intently as Adrian and JJ interacted with each other. The other speakers were stodgy—some were downright boring. But Adrian and JJ were different. They had a real, palpable affection for one another.

"I wasn't even going to run for national office," Adrian said.

"That's right, not until you met those Bros..." JJ began.

"...from Mu Chapter!" they said in unison, chuckling together.

"I had been through a lot in my first year as a Brother, personally and in the frat. A lot of Brothers don't know this, but I had a real-life bully in my chapter. It went so far beyond hazing that it was frightening. And I had always known, intellectually, that being a gay man in a fraternity wasn't necessarily the safest decision for me to make. But I also felt like if Brothers knew who I was on the inside, my orientation wouldn't matter." He stole a glance at JJ and continued.

"But it did matter to this one Brother, and we ultimately suspended him from the chapter."

The crowd gasped.

"See, that's what y'all don't know about Adrian. He has always been about knowing the rules. Now whether he follows them-"

"Is not up for debate," Adrian laughed. The Brothers in the crowd followed.

"But seriously," JJ said.

"Yes, seriously. Because of those experiences as well as my chapter being put on investigation later that year, I knew something had to give in the frat. So I ran for office. And I won."

The audience clapped, none more vigorously than JJ.

"Now Adrian didn't tell you that he ran unopposed. But like six, seven brothers ran for undergraduate member at large, and I won by like three votes. But a win is a win, right?" JJ smiled.

"Questions from the audience?" the moderator asked. My hand shot up. After I was acknowledged, I rose.

"Ian Kenney, Pi Chapter, Spring 2014…"

"Congrats, neo!" Adrian smiled.

"Thank you, Brother Collins. My question for you and JJ: it's been 15 years since your initiation, and maybe a dozen years since your term on the national board. What are some of the defining moments of your friendship and brotherhood?"

"Wow, excellent question, Brother Ian," Adrian said.

"Yeah, they making these neos smarter and smarter," JJ smiled.

"I think the experience we've had on the board together was pretty defining by itself, but it's truly the moments outside of the fraternity that matter most. For me, it was probably my wedding day. JJ was one of my groomsmen. I'll just say it like this: you wouldn't find too many men in 2003 who would have stood up for another man in a gay wedding, and even serenade his husband. But JJ and many other Brothers did that for me."

The room erupted into chatter and light applause.

"And for me, it was my graduation from Georgetown Law in 2006. I'd had…" JJ stopped, closed his eyes, and put the microphone down for a moment.

"Take your time," Adrian whispered, the microphone catching his words.

"My last year in law school was the most trying time of my life. I was going through a lot personally. And when I thought I was all alone, there was Adrian. Texting me every day to make sure I was okay, going to class, going to the library. A lot of those days, I wasn't okay. But Adrian did what he had to do as a Brother to make sure that I was. That's why, next to my parents and my wife, he will always have a prominent seat at my table. Without his counsel, I wouldn't be a lawyer at all."

JJ's eyes streamed with tears. Adrian wiped away a tear of his own.

Those were not insignificant tears or an insignificant set of circumstances. These men loved each other. I found myself also tearing up.

The panel went on, but I fixated on the stories from the late 90s and early 00s, Adrian and JJ's era. My chapter wasn't even visited by men from that period. The oldest alumni I'd met were from 2010 at the earliest.

As the panel closed, I made a beeline for the stage.

"Brother Collins, Brother Carter? Ian Kenney, Pi Chapter. I was wondering if you had any plans right now?"

"Right now? Can't say that I do," Adrian said.

"Me either. Well, except going to the bar," JJ added.

"Care to join us?" Adrian asked.

"Wait, are you even 21?" JJ asked.

"Yes, sir. Definitely 21."

"Then yes, come join us. You look like you've got something on your mind, good brother."

I followed them through the hotel lobby as they chatted away about old times. We settled into a booth at the bar and, at Adrian's insistence, I began talking.

"I know you don't know me-"

"You're a Brother. That's all we need to know," JJ interjected.

"Thank you. And I'd appreciate it if what I'm about to tell you remains confidential."

"Sure thing," Adrian said.

"My chapter…well, my line…it's hard to explain. Basically, my chapter didn't want most of us. They had the five they wanted, but six more were added on. I was one of the six."

"Damn, that's still going on?" JJ said.

"Happened to us, too—it just depends on how you handle it," Adrian reminded JJ.

"Well, we're not handling it at all."

"What's happening?" JJ asked.

"Our prophytes are treating us like shit, therefore our LBs who were 'chosen' are now also treating us like shit."

"What does that look like?" Adrian asked. I pulled out my cell phone and brought up my chapter's Instagram account.

"These are photos from our probate. Notice anything?"

Adrian and JJ scrolled through.

"Yep. Some of you are in black jackets. Some of you are in white. And there are a lot more candid shots of those of you in white jackets," JJ deduced.

"And that's just what the public sees. Our line names are all screwed up. I found out they call me 'Skintight' because they said I got squeezed in to the frat."

"Ouch," Adrian said.

"I'm not trying to snitch on my chapter. But I feel like the six of us are good dudes who want to do the work of the fraternity. How can we do that when they keep excluding us?"

"This is nuts," JJ said.

"Yet it's not new. Listen, when I was in school, even my line of seven had those who were wanted and those the chapter had to take. And it happened to the line after us, too."

"What about you, Brother Carter?" I asked.

"Not so much with Alpha Chapter. We didn't play that. Brothers we didn't want knew not to show up."

I winced.

"No offense."

"We worked through it. I learned how to empathize with those who were feeling neglected, and they learned how to ease themselves into the chapter so their hard work would be noticed," Adrian said.

"I think we might be a little further past that level of reason." JJ said, leaning back in his seat.

"I agree. These guys are borderline humiliating them to the public. I don't know that you can negotiate with people like that," Adrian said.

"But negotiation is really all you have," JJ continued. "Listen, I know HBCU chapters are different. But fundamentally, you're dealing with people of a certain age trying to answer the question 'Who runs the yard?' It's a dumb question, but that's the tipping point here. Everything we do leads to who's got the juice on campus at the end of the day. I think you already know that telling your chapter advisor or region director is an option, but is it the option that leads to you running the yard?"

"No. If we say something to them, we'll be investigated. It would be cutting off my nose to spite my face."

"Correct," Adrian said. "But can you talk to these brothers? Can you, through your words and your deeds, convince them that your half of the line is just as dope?"

"I don't know."

"Maybe you should try. Your journey is going to be different from mine and from JJ's, which were different from each other. And your journey might even be different from everybody else in your chapter. But you're here. Now."

"Do you have a mentor?" JJ asked.

I shook my head.

"I don't. I have a few cool professors, but I don't have a mentor in my field."

"What's your field?" Adrian asked me.

"I want to be a pharmacist," I said.

"Hmm," Adrian said, looking at JJ.

"You already know," JJ said to Adrian.

"What do you mean?" I asked.

"Listen, little brother, I have somebody in mind that I think you should link up with. Professionally, you've got nothing in common. But he's one of the best Betas that I know. You need a mentor. And he doesn't know it yet, but he needs a mentee."

"Miles?" Adrian asked. JJ scoffed.

"No. Eustace." Adrian paused and pondered the idea. "Oh. You know what? Yep. Here for it."

"Eustace Dailey? The photographer? Genius grant?"

"One in the same," JJ said.

"You're going to introduce me to Eustace Dailey?!"

"I'm not. I don't even have his number anymore. But Adrian does. Adrian, will you make the introduction for our dear little brother Ian?"

"Absolutely. I agree with you. This is a match."

Adrian pulled out his phone, found Eustace's number, and called him. After a few moments of chatter, Adrian got to the point.

"Eustace, listen. Need a favor. I've got a young brother here from Morehouse who needs a mentor. Now before you say no...listen...reminds me of you when you were his age. Smart. Idealistic. But taller and leaner. I want you to stay with him through his graduation. That's less than a year from now. You don't even gotta ever see him. Just talk to him every once in a while, make sure he's good. Eustace...hello? Oh, okay, thought I lost you. Sure, hold on." He paused and passed the phone to me.

"He wants to speak to you."

I took a hard swallow of my drink and took the phone.

"Hello Brother Dailey, my name is Ian Kenny."

"Brother Ian, I have some questions to ask you. Smile and nod with each question, okay?" Eustace said.

I smiled and nodded.

"Yes, sir!"

"Don't call me sir, please. First and foremost, did you seek me out through Adrian because you think a friendship with me will elevate your lifestyle?"

I smiled and shook my head.

"Not at all, Brother Dailey. Didn't expect to be on the phone with you. They invited me over."

"They? Are there two men there with you?"

"Yes."

"Is one of them JJ Carter?"

"Absolutely."

"Was this mentorship his idea?"

"It was. Would you like to-"

"No. I would not like to speak to him. Are you smiling and nodding?"

"Yes, I am."

"Do you want me to be your mentor?"

"Yes. I do."

"Then consider it done. Put Adrian back on the phone. Talk to you soon."

"Thank you, Brother Dailey!" I handed the phone back to Adrian.

"Yes, Eustace. No, Eustace. *No* Eustace. I got you. I will. Goodbye."

He ended the call and put his phone back in his pocket.

"Eustace said hello," he said to JJ, who smiled slightly.

"Thank you," he told Adrian softly.

"Well kid, looks like you've got yourself a Beta mentor! Now listen. He's busy—in fact, he's a hurricane—but he's committed. He takes our word for it that you're worth it. And you are. So don't change, except for the better. Got it?"

"Got it. Thank you so much, Brothers."

"Now this shit with your chapter ain't gonna get better overnight. And Eustace isn't a miracle worker. But if you need somebody to talk to, you can count on him. And us. Okay?"

"Okay. Thank you so much. You just don't know how much this means to me."

Eustace came to Atlanta that September, right after move-in weekend. He had an assignment in town and made time to see me. We met at Aurora Coffee in Little Five Points, a small shop with tall walls adorned with abstract and surreal art on one side and leaflets and fliers on the other.

He was taller than I imagined, but not as tall as me. Let's face it—I was lanky. All arms and legs. Eustace was a handsome dude. He looked like he could be as a good a model as he was a photographer. Broad shoulders, huge biceps, a thin waist, and bulging thighs. I could have easily mistaken him for a member of the Atlanta Falcons. He had a handsome face, too, with a kinky afro and facial hair to match.

And I had seen his work. His portraits were legendary. White folks called him the next Herb Ritts. Black folks called him the next Gordon Parks. I just called him "Frat."

"Ian!" he called out from a table in the far corner of the coffee shop. I smiled, waved, and hurried to him.

"It's so good to meet you face to face," I said.

"Same here. Come on, have a seat." I sat my bookbag in the booth and took a seat across from him.

"What brings you to town?" I asked.

"JD wants me to do a shoot for some of his new artists, so I've got studio space all day tomorrow."

"JD? As in Jermaine Dupri?" I asked.

"Yeah, him."

"Whoa…that's crazy."

"It's work, know what I mean?"

"Yeah, but everybody doesn't get that kind of work."

"I'm just lucky, I guess. How do you take your coffee?" he asked as the server came by.

"Oh, uh, one cream, one sugar," I said.

"And two sugars, no cream for me, please," he said. The server nodded and scurried off.

"Adrian told me about your chapter. How are y'all doing currently?"

"About the same, if not worse. Not even really speaking to each other outside of chapter meeting at this point."

"Damn. That's too bad. What are you going to do about it?"

"Nothing. The 'Odds" are imploding. Half are begging to be post-pledged. The other half doesn't even wear letters on campus anymore."

"And what about you?"

"I worked hard for mine. I wear my letters and I go to chapter meetings. If they want to call me Skintight, fine. But let the reason be that ain't nobody in the chapter gonna be tighter than me."

"Good enough. You're graduating in May anyway, right?"

"Absolutely. I need to find some kind of internship or fellowship, though. I'm going to take a year off before I go to Pharmacy school."

"That sounds like a good plan. I didn't go to grad school right away, myself. I worked for a few years before I went."

"What kind of work did you do?"

"I was a management consultant for Concord, in DC."

"Oh, so you were down there at the same time Brother JJ was there for law school?" Eustace paused and nodded.

"Yes. We were there at the same time. I left six months before he did."

"That's crazy. Betas are everywhere."

"Yeah, but the northeast is different. Beta chapters up there pledge together, road trip together, have joint step teams. We have a tight bond before we even graduate, and when we do, we even migrate together."

"I can dig it. I kinda can't wait to get away from my chapter," I laughed.

"I wish I had better advice for you."

"No, bruh. It's fine. You, JJ, and Adrian have shown me what brotherhood is all about. Maybe I was never meant for undergrad life."

"Don't say that. A lot can change in a year. One email from the University of New Mexico turned my whole life upside down. When I left DC, I left a lot of…situations. Things I needed to leave behind to grow. A decade and some change later, I don't even know if I recognize who I was back then," he laughed.

"It's hard to visualize a future where I don't recognize my past," I said.

"Maybe your future won't be like that. You have a much firmer plan than I had at your age. Why pharmacy?"

Our mugs of coffee arrived and I slowly sipped mine.

"My grandma had a lot of health problems—she died in hospice when I was nine. I remember a lot of people in the health field were friendly to her and helped her out. And they were friendly to us, too. Nobody ever talked over us or around us about her. Her neighborhood pharmacist saw her regularly and knew her on a first name basis, too. I saw him whenever we made store runs. He was at her funeral and everything. When I looked up what pharmacists did, it sounded really interesting and fun and not as stressful as medicine or surgery."

"That's cool, bro. I didn't roll with science nerds too much in college. My crew was into the liberal arts, law, business…shit like that."

"What was Harvard like?" I asked.

"It was good. A lot of work. Stressful. Cold as shit in the winter. But I had a great time."

"You didn't want to go to an HBCU?"

"Not really. I wanted to be in the Northeast."

"Why?"

"Young and dumb. I wanted that Boston/New York/Philly vibe. Rugby shirts and pea coats. I had a narrow view of what college was supposed to look like."

"In spite of *A Different World?*" I laughed. He joined me.

"Truth be told…I wasn't sure that being black and openly gay was gonna work at an HBCU."

"You're gay?" I asked. He nodded.

"And now that I'm older, I know I would have been fine. But when you're 17, 18, no matter how proud you are, some debates you don't want to entertain. And for the most part, at Harvard, I never had any problems being black and gay. I wasn't the only one."

"I can understand that. I mean, I'm not gay, but I've got a few gay Morehouse brothers that don't necessarily have it easy all the time."

"It's tough. But we've all got our own crosses to bear. Hold on a second, I have to take this call real quick."

I sipped my coffee. How did I not know Eustace Dailey was gay? Had I been under a rock? I knew Adrian was gay. Was JJ? Nah, he had a wife and kids. Jesus, I hope I didn't offend him somehow.

"Dammit," he said.

"What's up?"

"The assistant I use in Atlanta had to go out of town for the weekend."

"Really?"

"Yeah. I can't lie, I'm super particular about who gets to work closely with me. And JD's an awesome client, but I don't like his staff that much. Shit."

"What does an assistant do for you? Want me to help you find a substitute?"

"All he or she has got to do is stand there and take direction. Move lights. Carry equipment. Read the meters. Wait...you could do that."

"I could? I mean, yeah, I could! Wait, really?"

"Do you want to? Are you free tomorrow?"

"Yeah. I'm definitely free tomorrow."

"Then it's done. Can you meet me at the studio at 9am?"

"Wow, Brother Dailey...I would love to do this. This is crazy!"

"Please...Brother Eustace is fine. Or just Eustace. I'm glad you're available. This should be fun."

And fun it was. I spent all day being Eustace's flunky, but it was so worth it. JD was amazing to observe in his own environment with all his proteges present. Some of his old artists swung through as well. It was a hip-hop who's who in there!

Eustace was the eye of the storm, directing each artist with precision for their portraits. He was a quiet force, easily getting into his artistic zone without alienating his subjects. They calmly obeyed his directions, hoping that their portrait would be *the one*—the next world-famous Eustace Dailey shot.

He showed me the raw images on his laptop well into Saturday night. We'd spent over twelve hours together by that point, but it was well worth it to see the images.

"Frat...these are beautiful. Wow."

"And you helped. Look at you."

"Naw, bruh. That's all you. Wow."

"Thank you. JD will be happy."

My phone vibrated. I read the series of frantic text messages.

"Brother Eustace...are we done here?"

"You need to go, li'l bro?"

I nodded my head vigorously.

"I'm sorry. This has been an amazing experience. Thank you for inviting me. I'll never forget it."

I hugged him and gave him the fraternal grip.

"Is everything okay? You look like you've seen a ghost."

"I'm fine. Everything's fine. I'll text you tomorrow, okay?"

I ran out and drove straight to Emory University Hospital Midtown.

When I arrived at the emergency room, three of my line brothers were in the waiting room. All three looked like they just got back from war.

"What the fuck happened?" I hissed. None looked at me.

"Answer me!" I said, getting louder.

"Yo, chill. I'm 'bout to tell you," Number Three said.

"I'm listening."

"We...four of us...four of the odds...we got approached to post-pledge. And we all said yes."

"Wow. So that's how it is?"

"It ain't got nothing to do with you, bro. They just don't...they don't see it for you, man. They never did. But they got to know us and wanted to give us a chance."

"So that's why y'all have been distant the past few weeks. Trying to have your own process so you'd be good by Homecoming," I deduced.

"Who wants to be trying to sing the hymn on the yard at Homecoming and have dozens of niggas looking at you crazy because nobody thinks you're 'real' Pi? That's why we did it. But shit got crazy, bruh. We been up since yesterday. Reciting shit. Getting hazed the fuck up. Then Ace snapped. He said he had enough. He tried to leave. Some old head blocked his path. And he started swinging and didn't stop."

"Then the Bruhs jumped us," Number 7 interjected. "Like, it was not even off no 'Control your boy' type shit. It was straight 'We finna kill y'all tonight' status. Like, who does that, man? What kinda people wait for the moment when they can start beating your ass? Why invite us to post-pledge in the first place?"

"Where's Jeff?" I asked.

"Jeff ain't get invited to join us."

"Then where's Kwame?"

"He's in surgery. They broke his jaw."

My heart sank.

"Where...the fuck...are they...right now?" I asked through clenched teeth. They all shrugged.

"What are we supposed to do now?" my line brother asked.

From that point forward, my senior year became the biggest blur out of all four years at Morehouse. Things happened all at once, in slow motion yet in hyper speed.

First, I did the worst thing somebody could do in a fraternity: I called the police.

Yup. I sure did. Whether or not I did it out of spite for not being a chosen one is immaterial. My line brother had a broken jaw. Somebody was going to go to jail for that.

After I called the police, I called the chapter advisor, like I was supposed to. He came to the hospital and sat with me and my line brothers all night, and well into the morning, when my line brother's parents came.

That's it. That's all. I did what I was supposed to do when a fucking crime happens. I told the truth.

The fallout was epic.

Because all my prophytes were present when the incident occurred, Morehouse expelled them all. They were subsequently expelled from Beta Chi Phi.

Kwame left Morehouse and went back home to Gary, Indiana, to recover. He later transferred to Indiana State. His family sued the fraternity and the school. Both settled out of court. I never knew the whole story, but word on the street was that the family got less than six figures.

The other line brothers who had been present were suspended by the fraternity for consenting to hazing. Beta always took the stance that one couldn't haze people who didn't show up, so if you showed up and agreed to what happened—always the case in post-pledging—then you, too, could get in trouble.

All the offenders were locked up for the weekend. Most plead guilty to hazing charges and got fines and probation. The ringleaders—the chapter president and the Dean of Pledges—chose to fight the charges. They lost. The president got six months in prison. The Dean—the one who threw the blow that broke my LB's jaw—he got 18 months.

But that was the aftermath, and much of it happened when I left Atlanta. The incident left Pi Chapter with two members: Jeff and me.

We begged, pleaded, and groveled to Morehouse and to Beta to save our chapter. We wrote letters. Sent references. Showed them our stellar grades. Showed them evidence that we had not consented to being hazed and, in fact, were not present at the incident.

I was even able to get the presidents of all the fraternities and social fellowships at Morehouse to send letters on our behalf. I would be graduating in May and I wanted desperately to have a real fraternity experience, even if it was just me and Jeff doing service and sponsoring small programs.

Finally, days before the Thanksgiving break, Morehouse relented and allowed Pi Chapter to return on a probationary basis, so long as me and Jeff were in charge, and no other members participated in any way.

That was fine by us. Jeff let me be President, as he'd have another full year after me to serve.

In December, we hosted a study break, held a coat drive for Fickett Elementary School, and had a yard show to remind the public that despite what they may have heard, Pi Chapter was still here. It was just the two of us, but we stepped our hearts out to the applause of our friends and supporters.

In January, we requested permission to have membership intake, and the school approved, with conditions including total oversight by our alumni chapter.

We agreed.

When it was time for rush, a record 70 men came out. We selected the best of them, by the book. Not even one of them had a

GPA below a 3.5. Attendees included organization presidents, class officers, and men who we were certain would be Rhodes Scholars.

All together, we chose 20—the best line in chapter history, and the largest in the modern era. Most of them were sophomores.

We brought them in the right way. We told them our stories. We told them our mistakes. We let them know that they were loved and wanted, but that they would have to work to rebuild the chapter's legacy.

We were honest with them. People would call them paper. Prophytes would likely ignore them all together, or try to convince them that they needed to post-pledge. We told them we knew it would be hard, but it's always hard being a pioneer.

These are lessons we instilled every day that the alumni chapter was committed to reinforcing.

Through it all, on a weekly basis, I checked in with my mentor. No matter where he was in the world, he made time to talk with me and to me. I navigated waters that were uncharted, and I often taught Eustace something new about the way things were done now.

I talked to Adrian, too, and JJ. We spoke less frequently, but I was convinced that their intercession is what led to Pi Chapter's early reinstatement. I invited them to Pi Chapter's New Member Presentation. Adrian and Eustace were able to attend.

Our boys were lit. 20 men in black pea coats and burgundy berets, khaki slacks, and identical black shoes, like the old days. They walked in silence and unison to the front of Kilgore, to a massive crowd. We were exhausted, but ready.

Since it was March 14, 2015, we dubbed the day Pi Day, matching perfectly with our chapter. Pi alumni from the 80s and 90s came out in large numbers to support us. But no brothers there mattered more to me than Adrian and Eustace—my mentor, my friend—who had come from miles away to lend a hand. Eustace, to my surprise, had his camera in hand.

I knew when I saw that camera that this day would be something special.

Our neos, who we dubbed "The Awakening," were perfect. Their 20 voices sounded more like 80 as they echoed across the yard.

Their show had many elements from the old days of Pi Chapter, traditions that had been lost over the years. More singing, less stepping. More humor, less gritting. Professionalism over disses. The invited prophytes were pleased.

But they did step and stroll. And they did introduce themselves one at a time with their line names—all uplifting and positive.

At the end, we sang the hymn with every ounce of passion we had left. I looked around the circle of well over a hundred men and realized that this was the Beta I had pledged for. Not the Beta that I got—but the Beta I had helped to create.

"What's next, li'l bro?" Eustace asked me as we sat on the yard, well after the show had ended.

"I dunno, bruh. I've thinking about this pharm tech internship program in New York."

"New York! That would be dope!"

"I can't afford to live in New York, though. So I'm looking at jobs in Atlanta."

"Is this thing in New York your number one choice, though?"

"Yeah."

"You got any problem with living in Brooklyn?"

"Brooklyn's aight. I got no problems with it."

"Then stay with me for the summer. My place is huge. I travel a lot and I wouldn't mind somebody checking the mail when I'm not there."

"Are you kidding me?"

"No, I'm not. Come to New York. Save some money. Help me out every once in a while."

I immediately began tearing up.

"No, no, none of that," he said.

"I can't help it. After all I went through in this organization, it just feels real good to experience this kind of brotherhood."

"Brotherhood is a verb. It's something you have to work on from the day you cross until the day you die. You're part of us and we're part of you. Don't forget to pay it forward when it's your turn, aight?"

I nodded through the tears.

"Aight. Thank you, bruh."

When I started college, I knew who I was and what I wanted to be. I thought I knew how to get there. By the time I graduated college, I knew to whom I belonged, where I belonged, and I had learned that it's never a straight line to get there.

Because of this brotherhood, I found my mentor, Eustace Dailey, a man who should have been my polar opposite. He was the artist to my scientist, the dreamer to my pragmatist, the elder to my youthful ways. He was gay and I was straight, but it never once came between us. When you have found the big brother you've always wanted, such things are irrelevant.

Chapter Five:
JJ

My wife sat in her usual early morning spot at the kitchen table while I made lunch for our children. The clock on the microwave read 6:15am. I'd have to wake them soon.

"JJ...what exactly is an eight-year-old going to do in Barbados for a week with six grown men?" I sat at the round table across from her.

Sylvia sipped her tea and glared at me over her reading glasses. She closed her Bible and laid it next to her notepad and teacup.

"He's not going to be with six random grown men. He's going to be with his father, his five uncles, and his cousin Zion."

"He's never even met some of those people. And Zion is 16. You think he wants to babysit a kid for a week while his 'uncles' are partying?"

"We're not even those kinds of people, Sylvia. You know that."

"Do I? The last two times I saw Eustace, he was so drunk he couldn't even stand up straight."

"That was eleven years ago. He's more than gotten his life together since then."

"So he has. But have you?"

Sylvia sipped her tea slowly. I stared at her without flinching.

"Three Jay deserves this. He busts his ass at school. He worries himself sick over his schoolwork. I want to show him how to have a good time doing nothing for a change. No soccer practice. No Boy Scouts. No homework. Just chillin' on a beach with his dad and the boys."

"Ian Kenney. That's the young man living with Eustace now, right?"

"Yes. The pharmacy student."

"This is the same one who got fired from his program over the summer because he was too hungover to make it to work on time? The same one who Eustace is basically letting live in his house-"

"Sylvia-"

"...rent free until he gets his life together?"

"He's just a 23 year old kid-"

"Eustace likes them young now?"

"What is your problem with Eustace all of a sudden? You know I don't hang out with him. I don't even call him, text him, nothing."

"So why be on an island with him now? Hm?"

"He's my friend. He always will be."

"Just remember who your friends were during your last year in law school when you almost flunked out."

Don't engage. Don't engage. Don't engage.

"So, look. You obviously have a problem with me taking this trip. Yet I'm taking this trip. If you have a problem with me taking our son, I'll leave him here. But I'm going on the trip."

She placed her teacup back on the saucer.

"This boy...Ian Kenney...he'll be babysitting our son?"

"Yes. He'll take care of Zion and Three Jay anytime I'm not there. But I'm telling you I'll be there."

"Fine." She opened her Bible and read it in silence.

"Thank you, Sylvia."

"You're welcome, dear."

I stood and walked away from the table.

"And JJ?"

"Yes?"

"Be safe."

I paused and turned to her. She stared me right in the eyes.

"I will be."

I walked down the long hallway to the stairs of our home. When it came to the men in my life, especially Betas, everything was a negotiation. It didn't matter how common or how exceptional they were. She didn't care whether you were the husband of a professional athlete or a world-famous photographer. She just didn't trust the Bros.

I walked up one stair and paused, removing my vibrating phone from my pocket. Grindr notified me of a new message.

WASSUP WIT U, PA?

The sender was a naked-chested, deep-brown skinned black man. The photo was cropped at his neck.

FACE PIC? I replied. I slowly walked to the top of the stairs. The phone vibrated again. I looked down and saw a reasonably handsome dude looking back at me. He'll do.

I unlocked all of my photos, from the dick pics to the face pics.

MEET ME AT THE MCDONALD'S ON LYNNWAY IN 30.

I held my phone in my hand as I entered my son's room.

"Three Jay. Wake up, buddy. Time for school."

"Morning," My son stretched his arms and groggily greeted me.

"Good morning, buddy," I responded. Before I woke my girls, I got a final message.

BET. SEE YOU SOON, PA.

I exhaled.

Chapter Six:
Eustace

I'm not one of those people who sits around and over-analyzes fraternalism, but it's not lost on me that over forty years ago, five men in Boston came together to start a new organization; and there was something about that organization that attracted five *different* men to it— a whole generation later.

Something attracted me to Beta, even though Harvard doesn't recognize fraternities, and nowadays seems to do everything it can to undermine fraternal organizations and the students who join.

My decision to pledge connected me to JJ, who had joined across town at Beta's mother chapter two years prior. Meanwhile, down in DC at the same time, our Brother Adrian was himself transforming into a Beta man.

The three of us would be joined by two more: Miles, my special brother that I had personally ushered in to my alumni chapter; and Ian, who had joined our brotherhood the latest of us all, but needed it the most.

I should have felt comfortable among these brothers. But to tell the truth, no matter how much time and distance separated all of us, the idea of being in the same space as JJ again after so much time had passed had me feeling as queasy as the last time I'd seen him.

"You good, Bruh?" Ian asked as the plane taxied toward the gate in Barbados.

"Yeah...I'm good. Glad we landed."

"You really don't like flying, huh?" he asked.

"It's a necessary evil." I sighed.

"But we here! Yo, I can't believe we in Barbados!"

"You're just on the runway. Wait until you feel that sunshine."

I'd never been to Barbados, but I'd been all across the Caribbean on various assignments earlier in my career. I'd shot beautiful models in the British Virgin Island for the *Sports Illustrated* Swimsuit Edition. I shot a French soccer player's engagement photos on Guadeloupe. I'd even done some architectural photography for a new resort in the Dominican Republic.

But Barbados...for fun...with frat. This was new.

"Don't forget your camera," Ian said as he dragged his wheeled carry-on down the aisle.

"Never." I pulled my camera bag from the overhead compartment and quickly slung it on my back.

We found our way to baggage claim and waited for the conveyor belt to engage. Ian chatted nonstop about everything he wanted to do over the next week, from drinking to parasailing.

"Don't forget Zion and Three Jay," I said.

"I won't be drunk the *whole* time, Bruh. I'ma be sober enough to take them for a walk or two."

I smirked at him and grabbed my bag off the belt. He quickly followed.

We walked toward the exit and found an older black guy around my height with a white sign saying "Dailey & Kenney."

"We sound like a law firm," Ian joked. I laughed.

"Hi, I'm Eustace Dailey and this is Ian Kenney," I told the man with the sign.

"Welcome to Barbados!" he exclaimed.

"Thank you so much!" Ian said, grabbing the man by his free hand and bringing him in for a hug.

"First time for both of you?" he asked. Ian nodded his head vigorously.

"Well you are in for a treat, my friends. I'm Jack, and I'll be taking you to your home for the week. It's a marvelous property right on Mullins Beach. Mr. Collins picked it out himself."

"Is that right?" I asked.

"Absolutely. Come, let me take your bags. The house is about 45 minutes from here."

Jack took our bags and walked us outside to our black town car.

"Dope," Ian said.

Jack let us into the car and we got comfortable in the cool air. We pulled off, driving right into the lush, green terrain surrounding the airport.

Barbados was beautiful in every way, from the sunshine to the shadows of the trees; from the washed out pastel paint covering the stores, to the beautiful brown people walking through the marketplaces. Although the town car was well air-conditioned, I rolled the window down to feel the sticky heat on my face. When Jack rolled to a stop at various points along the way, I snapped a few photos as well.

After a while, we pulled off Highway 1B and onto a private driveway that circled a small fountain. The two-story house—truly a magnificent villa—was perfectly framed by huge palm trees. Its gray stone exterior seemed to soar into the sky, up to a pointed roof with ornate trim. The main building was flanked by two wings, and each disappeared into masses of palm trees.

Adrian and Zion stood on the stairs waiting for us. Zion was easily taller than Adrian by a few inches already—and he looked uncannily like his father did when he was younger.

They approached the car and opened the doors for us. We stepped onto the red brick driveway.

"Welcome to Barbados!" Zion said to Ian while shaking his hand.

"Thank you, young sir! Wow…is this where we're staying?!"

"It's dope!" Zion said.

"Wait until you see the pool," Adrian said while gripping Ian. He turned his attention to me.

"My brother," I said.

"Baby bro," Adrian responded. We eschewed the fraternal handshake entirely and hugged. It had been too long since we'd last seen each other.

"You look great! I am loving this afro and beard," Adrian said, rubbing his fingers over my hair.

"Thank you. I call it the 'too busy for a haircut' look."

"Well it's awesome. Come on in, guys. You're the first to arrive."

Adrian led us into the villa where we were amazed at every turn by the size and beauty. We passed through several sitting areas and finally arrived at the humongous pool, which seemed to stretch its blue waters all the way to the horizon.

At poolside, Adrian had for us all the brunch foods we could desire: bacon, sausage, French toast, scrambled eggs, fresh fruit, and mimosas.

"Eat. Drink. Be merry. Please." Adrian instructed.

Ian's eyes grew huge.

"Not all at once, li'l bro." He relaxed a bit and excused himself to wash his hands.

"I miss you, Uncle Eu," Zion said as he put his arm around my shoulder.

"I miss you, too, boy," I said with a smile.

"Why you never visit us?"

"You know I travel a lot for work. And when I'm not traveling, I've got back to back shoots in New York."

"You know what you should do, Uncle Eu?"

"What?"

"You should let me be your apprentice next summer!"

"Help me with photo shoots?"

"Yes! That's the kind of summer experience that could get me into a great college."

"So you don't think you'll get into Potomac without a cool summer job?"

"Being a double-legacy don't take you as far as it used to," Adrian grumbled. He took a seat by the pool with his mimosa. I joined him.

"Somehow, Zion, I think you're more interested in the female models I work with than the art of photography."

"Hey…what's wrong with caring about both?" he laughed.

Adrian and I chuckled and shook our heads in tandem.

"Zion, why don't you show Ian to his room?" Adrian suggested.

"No doubt, Papa," he said as he picked up Ian's bag and scurried off. Their voices echoed as they disappeared into the house.

"He looks like his dad," I confessed to Adrian.

"Yeah…but I see his mom, too."

I sighed.

"It never gets easier, does it?"

"It's a strange kind of grief. Isaiah loved her once, so his grief is tinged with guilt. Zion never knew her, though. When he asks questions about her, he genuinely wants to know what kind of person she was, what she liked and disliked, what her voice sounded like. His grief is like a sadness wrapped in curiosity."

"And your grief?"

"I don't know that I grieved for her. Her death was so sudden. Zion came to us so quickly—in spite of Jamal and his ridiculous custody case."

"What a lunatic."

"I mean, I get it. He was as alone and adrift as Taina. But he wasn't crazy. He was evil. Had he not been so fixated on ruining me and Isaiah, he would have seen that Taina was bipolar and needed help."

"And you and Isaiah were so separated from her, you wouldn't have known what was going on."

"Taina hated me at first. The hatred cooled to resentment, but she never really liked me. What would she have shown me other than what she wanted me to see? That she was strong and had it all together."

Adrian sipped his mimosa, as did I. He continued.

"I shudder to think what would have happened if Taina had put Zion in her jeep the night of the crash. I don't know what my life would be like without that boy."

"I think no matter how far gone she was, no matter how depressed and suicidal she was, there was always one shred of sanity in her. And thank God that shred kept Zion safe."

"Thank God," Adrian said, clinking glasses with me. "Nina asked about you, by the way," he added.

"Oh yeah? How's she?" Adrian's phone began to vibrate.

"Oh, Miles is near. Let's go out front," Adrian said. We rose from poolside and walked back through the house to the driveway.

Miles' driver opened the door for him and he stepped out, wearing a simple black suit and white collared shirt with no tie. He wore mirrored aviator sunglasses. When he saw us, he snatched them off and smiled. His perfect teeth stretched from ear to ear. It was startling to see him with a trendier haircut rather than dreadlocks: curly and high on top, shaved to a fade at the sides, and topped off with frosty blue tips.

"Supermodel!" Adrian shouted.

"Of the world!" I said. Miles stretched his arms out and walked quickly to us, embracing us both at the same time.

"Brothers…it's been too long!" he said.

"You look amazing!" Adrian said.

"Thanks, bro. So do you both! Eustace, all this hair! I can't!"

I palmed my beard and smiled.

"Spesh. I am so glad to see you," I said. He grabbed my hand and held it.

"Me too, bro. Me too."

"Come in, grab something to eat," Adrian said.

"Don't mind if I do!" Miles said.

We settled into our relationships as quickly as we settled into our seats. I wanted to hear all about how Miles fared as the world's sexiest nerd.

"Bro, I can't believe I've been riding this train this long. I guess the world was waiting for a handsome librarian."

"No, not handsome," Adrian interrupted. "*People* called you sexy. There's a difference."

"You know how I do," he said quietly.

"How's Dr. Carly?" Adrian asked.

"She's amazing. Loving work. I don't get it, but I don't have to."

"Y'all are such a good match," I said.

"What about you, Bro?" Miles asked me.

"What about me?"

"You seeing anybody these days?"

I smiled, looked in the bottom of my empty mimosa glass, and looked away.

"No. I'm not seeing anybody."

"He too busy raising his son, Ian," Adrian quipped.

"Shut the hell up, Adrian," I laughed.

"Ian's the new kid, right?" Miles asked.

"He's a grown man and a prophyte already," I offered.

"He's 23, looks younger than Zion, and if you think Eustace isn't in love with him, I've got a bridge in Brooklyn to sell you," Adrian said.

"Why you coming for me! I am not attracted to Ian. And anyway, he's straight."

"That hasn't stopped you before," Miles deadpanned.

I slowly turned my head toward Miles only to find him sipping his mimosa with his pinky up.

"I'ma get you for that one, little brother," I menaced.

"Truth hurts, big brother," he retorted.

Voices echoed through the house once more and Zion and Ian reappeared.

"Yo, this place is dope! Oh, I'm sorry—Brother Miles! Pleased to meet you!"

"Bother Ian! The pleasure is all mine." They smiled, embraced, and performed the handshake.

"Well, this is it—for a while, at least," Adrian said.

"JJ not coming?" Miles asked.

"He and Three Jay will be in late tonight, after dinner," Adrian explained.

"I'm looking forward to seeing him again," Ian said.

"Indeed," Adrian said. "Well, Brothers. Make yourselves at home. Eat. Walk around the grounds. Most importantly, relax. We work hard every day, now it's time for peace and calm. Dinner will be served at 7pm. If you'd like to join me at Meeting in the morning, the car leaves at 9:30am. We'll be back here by noon."

"Brother Adrian, what meeting are you talking about?" Ian asked.

"Apologies. Meeting for worship. Friends meeting. The Quakers."

"You're a Quaker?" Ian asked.

"Yeah, for a few years now. We worship in silence. It's helped me relax."

"Word. I'll join you tomorrow," I said. Adrian smiled.

"Awesome. Well Brothers, enjoy the house! I'll see you this evening."

Dinner was an extravagant meal of all the best American fare: steak, lobster, potatoes, salad—real hearty food to replenish us after a long day of traveling. We laughed and joked about the old days. We listened to Ian's stories of his shenanigans in New York—some trouble I'd never even known he'd gotten into. Miles told us the salacious stories from Paris and Milan. And Adrian filled us in on what went on behind the scenes in professional sports and reality television, as well as the latest suspensions and drama in our beloved Beta Chi Phi.

"Brothers, I did have a small announcement to make. I can't wait until JJ arrives. Do you like this villa?"

"Damn straight," Miles said while we all nodded.

"Well, Isaiah bought it. It's ours. This is our house now."

"Nigga what!" I shouted.

"Jesus Christ!" Ian said.

"Wow," Miles added.

"You know we're blessed, and-"

"You bought a villa," I said.

"We came down here before, rented the house, loved it…"

"A whole villa," Miles added.

"And decided this is where we want to be when we're not in Baltimore."

"My frat owns this," Ian concluded in bewilderment.

"It's pretty amazing, isn't it? Imagine the graduation party!" Zion said.

"Now wait a minute," Adrian interjected. "That depends on whether or not you make the right choice in colleges."

"Yeah yeah yeah, 'Potomac Pirates, arrrrgh!'" Zion mocked.

"Anyway…so this is ours. To celebrate family, friendship, and brotherhood. No matter where you go in the world, know that the Aiken house is always your home."

"Cheers. And congratulations!" Miles said.

We lifted our glasses in celebration of Adrian's milestone. Such success couldn't have happened to a more deserving guy than him.

I scrolled through the photos I had taken during the day while sitting in my bed. Light knocks at my door penetrated the villa's otherwise silent wing.

"Come in." Miles entered. He was shirtless and wore loose gray cotton shorts over his tight, lime green boxer briefs. His Nike sandals clomped lightly on the floor as he walked toward me. His body glistened; every single muscle I remembered from his youth was present and well-defined.

I smiled.

"Hey, friend."

"Hey big bro." He smiled.

"Whatchu up to?"

"Nothing. Just wired. Good vibes, though."

"It's already an amazing vacation, isn't it?"

"It is. Hey, big bro, can I talk to you about something?"

"Sure. What's up?"

"I wanted to apologize for what I said earlier. About Ian being straight not stopping you."

"That? Please, frat, I wasn't offended at all. If I can't take teasing from y'all, I have no business being here."

"I hear you. Still, I was wrong. Honestly bro, I said that because of JJ, not because of you."

"What do you mean?"

"I worry about you."

"Me? Why?" I laughed.

"Eustace, stop. It's me you're talking to."

I paused.

"It's not going to be like it was before, Miles. Me and JJ are ancient history."

"When's the last time you saw him?"

"You know."

"Yes...I do. And I know the parting wasn't peaceful if you haven't spoken to him in a decade."

"It actually was peaceful. But I needed a clean break from him. Anyway, I'm not the same person. Hopefully, neither is he."

"Have you communicated with him at all?"

"You know I haven't—why are we doing this?"

"Because I want to make sure you're ready to see him. I don't want no relapses. No backsliding. JJ had you sprung like a Slinky."

"Miles, come on man. I've dated plenty over the years. Had friends. Had heartache. JJ is yesterday. I'm looking forward to meeting his..." I paused.

"Son?"

"His son. Yes."

"I promise you, Eustace. If JJ fucks with you this week...if he puts you through a bunch of bullshit again...I can't promise you I'ma be brotherly with him."

I smiled.

"Miles, you couldn't hurt an ant at a step show."

"And while that might be true...I want to look out for you like you looked out for me. You've been a great big brother. Let me be a great little brother."

"All you gotta do is keep being yourself, man. I can handle JJ."

"Aight..." he exhaled.

"But real talk, that's the most grown man thing I've ever seen. You coming in here making sure I'm good."

Miles smiled.

"But wear more clothes next time you bust in my room. You might not be gay, but I'm also not blind."

Miles flexed his pecs, laughed warmly, and nodded. "You got it, Bro."

I fell asleep with my camera on my nightstand. Voices down the hallway later roused me from my light sleep. I laid still and listened.

"Three Jay! Three Jay, this way!" JJ's gravelly voice tried to whisper.

Fast footsteps quickly got louder. The doorknob turned and my door flung open.

"Look at *this* room, Daddy!" the boy said. I kept my eyes shut.

"Sh! Quiet, Three Jay, people are sleeping!"

"Who's that, Daddy?"

JJ kept quiet for a few seconds.

"That's Mr. Eustace. He's Daddy's..."

His voice trailed off and never completed his sentence.

"Let's go, Three Jay." JJ closed the door quietly and walked back down the hall.

Later, I would wonder whether his description of me was incomplete after all.

Adrian, Ian, and I woke up before everyone else and headed over to the St. Michael Friends Meeting. Quakers didn't believe in saints—St. Michael was the name of the community.

All three of us seemed preoccupied and sat in relative silence as the car took a quick path to the meeting house. It was a small, unassuming building on an otherwise residential street in St. Michael.

The room's pews were arranged in a square, with empty space in the middle. The pews on the far walls were slightly elevated. Three members were already in the seats, in different spots throughout the room.

Ian and I sat in the third pew, and Adrian sat in front of us. We looked around for a moment, waiting for something to happen.

"Welcome to the St. Michael Friends Meeting," an older gentleman said from the front row. He stood up. "We are members of the Religious Society of Friends, better known as the Quakers. We worship in silence, in expectant waiting for God to speak directly to us and through us. From time to time, members will feel so moved as to share the testimony that they believe has been sent from God. John Yungblut said: 'If one has been visited by a direct sense of inward presence, he is driven to tell everyone who will listen to him.' We now welcome you to wait expectantly with us."

The man took his seat. As Adrian's head bowed, so did we.

I was not a church-goer. My parents found the black churches in St. Louis to be problematic for a young, outspoken gay boy and his family. We believed in God, but we didn't mesh well with organized religion.

Ironically, a core value of Beta Chi Phi was faith. Bible verses and Christian lore peppered our ritual, even though our actions in the pledge process were decidedly tangential to any sort of religious practices.

Because of this, I could understand why someone like Adrian would be attracted to the Quaker faith. If the fraternity was to be our entrance into lives of deeper faith, it was a poor start unless you already had a deep belief. For regular members like us, we'd eventually need more.

I needed more when I went through my battles with JJ, and even more when I went off to grad school without a single family member or friend in all of New Mexico. Instead of church, or even therapy, I threw myself into my photography, leaving it all in the camera.

It helped. Isolating myself from all but Adrian and Miles, ignoring JJ entirely, helped me heal from what I put myself through with him. They begged me to come visit, but I refused. Not until I got my MFA.

And when I got it, the work picked up. I knew what kind of photographer I wanted to be, but I also had to pay rent. There was no time to socialize. And if the brothers wanted to see me, they'd have to find me.

Adrian was the first to find me, in Chicago, when Isaiah's team played the Bulls. He never gave up. Texted me often. Insisted that I come out with him to the game. I did. It was like no time had passed at all. I was grateful to him for not giving up on me.

I saw Miles shortly thereafter, as his modeling career was taking off. He invited me to a shoot and introduced me to everyone there.

They knew me as the other half of our "Black John & Yoko" image and were interested in seeing how my career was developing.

Miles always put me in the mix, even when I wasn't sure I was ready to be there. From that visit alone, I started booking more fashion shoots.

And when Adrian and JJ called, they knew the missing piece in my life was somebody to mentor. If left to my own devices, I'd retreat and never turn back. But Ian's presence in my life was good for the both of us. He needed someone to look out for him. I needed someone to look out for. Without Ian at home, there might be days that I didn't even take a shower because I'd be so busy. Or so sad. At times.

Sitting here in this Quaker meeting, I reviewed all the things for which I was thankful and I became overwhelmed with this sense of gratitude.

It's not easy being my friend. They love me anyway.

I rocked back and forth in my seat, ever so slightly, moved by all I had been through with the help of my best friends.

A seat creaked at the other side of the meeting room as someone stood. I opened my eyes—a middle aged black lady had risen.

"I've been thinking a lot this week about the election in America. And I've been wondering to myself whether the average American understands that all eyes are on them right now. I wonder what they think and how they will vote. And it reminded me of the Bible verse from Corinthians, which goes 'it is required of stewards that one be found trustworthy.'

"My cousins who live in America always complain to me about the lack of trustworthy politicians. And I think the same way, here in Barbados. But what is a politician other than a person who wants to lead?

"And shouldn't we all want to lead? Our relationships? Our families? Our communities?

"We are all stewards, and therefore, we must all be trustworthy. And loyal. And kind. The politicians are us. And if they come from us, then maybe someday we can trust them."

The lady held the pew in front of her and sat. Adrian, Ian, and I closed our eyes once more.

This was true peace. I understood it. Adrian had a busy lifestyle, thanks to his husband's work. It made sense that he'd choose a faith tradition that allowed him the chance to sit still for an hour a week. I got it.

JJ.

I feared letting thoughts of him penetrate the silence. I didn't know what I needed to pray for when it came to him. Peace? Understanding? Love?

He'd made his choice. I had made mine. The story was over. The page had been turned. It was time to begin a new story.

But how could I begin a new story when my heart was stuck in 2005?

Ian nudged me. I opened my eyes and saw that his hand was extended to mine. I shook it.

"Is that it?" I whispered.

"I don't know. They just started shaking hands and saying 'good morning.'"

"Oh." I walked across the meeting house with Adrian and Ian and shook hands with the other attendees. We were thanked for coming. As the questions came, we explained that we were with Adrian and visiting for the week. In turn, he fielded the questions expertly, with all types of Quaker jargon I hadn't yet learned.

"How did you enjoy the meeting?" Adrian asked as we headed back to the car.

"It was…interesting," I said.

"Kinda cool," Ian contributed.

"It helps me focus for the week," Adrian said.

"Like meditation," Ian said. Adrian nodded.

"Thanks for coming with me, guys. It means a lot."

"If I had to be in a church on a Sunday morning in Barbados, this was a pretty cool one to be in." I smiled.

Adrian smiled back.

We got back to the villa and walked to the kitchen, where brunch waited for us, as were the boys Three Jay and Zion, and Miles and JJ.

"Finally, I can greet you in the light of day!" Adrian exclaimed. JJ stood and barreled over to Adrian, giving him a bear hug. Ian and I stood by quietly.

"What's up, Frat! How was Meeting?"

"It was good," Adrian smiled. JJ turned his attention to me.

"Eustace. It's been too long." He smiled. I didn't know what to say. I reached out my hand to him and he clasped it, bring me to his body. He wrapped me in his arms for the first time in eleven years.

"Too long," I repeated. I held him back. He was bigger. His goatee was longer and it even had a few premature gray hairs.

But he was JJ.

He released me and stood back a few feet.

"Wow. All this scruff. You look like...a real artist."

"He is a real artist," Miles interjected. JJ ignored him.

"This is Ian," I said.

"I know Ian," JJ responded. Of course he did. He met Ian before I did. Stupid.

"Good seeing you again, Brother JJ," Ian said, extending his hand to him.

"Eustace...this is my son. Jeremy Jacob Carter, Jr. Stand up, Three Jay."

The boy stood, his brown skin gleaming in the light pouring in through the kitchen window. He was the perfect combination of his parents: the gregarious, inquisitive visage of his father and the stately gait of his mother. His eyes, though, were all JJs.

"Hi, Mr. Eustace," he said. I extended my hand to him and he grabbed it as firmly as an eight-year-old could.

"It's nice to meet you. What should I call you?"

"Three Jay is fine!" he announced. He quickly sat again and turned his attention to his bagel.

"Wow," I whispered.

"Time...it goes on, with or without us," JJ muttered as he walked past me, reaching for paper towels on the kitchen counter.

"So we're all here now," Miles said.

"Yeah, so what's the plan, brotherman?" JJ asked Adrian.

"All plans are optional, my Brothers. But yes indeed, there are plans. If you want to take the jeep tour of the island, we're leaving here at 2pm. Then dinner on the beach."

"I'm in!" Ian exclaimed.

"So am I," Miles said.

"We're in," JJ said on behalf of his son.

"You coming, Uncle Eu?" Zion asked. I nodded.

"Yeah. I'm down."

The jeep tour was an excellent idea. The seven of us divided into two jeeps and explored the entire island with knowledgeable tour guides. We saw beaches, forests, hillsides, and markets. We were so engaged that I forgot to panic about seeing JJ again. I didn't neglect my camera, either. I captured beautiful shots of the people of Barbados—even more pictures of them than the stunning vistas.

By the time we returned to the villa, the bar had been well stocked by Adrian's staff.

"Help yourselves, gentlemen," Adrian said.

"Don't mind if I do," Ian said with a chuckle. He poured out shots of rum for all of us.

"Come on, bruhs. First shot in Barbados. Grab a glass."

Zion pulled out his phone and snapped pictures.

"Not for the 'Gram, please," JJ pleaded.

"My bad, Uncle JJ."

"It's all good. I just don't need to hear nothing from this one's mother."

Miles stared at JJ for a microsecond, then grabbed his own glass.

"A toast," Ian began. We held our shot glasses high.

"To our brotherhood. May it go on."

We clinked glasses and took the shots. They went down smoothly and I immediately loosened up.

"Whew!" JJ said. "Let me get the boy washed up for dinner. We'll be right back."

JJ and Three Jay disappeared upstairs, while Zion and Ian wandered poolside.

Miles leaned against the bar in the kitchen.

"You good, big bro?" he asked me. I nodded and looked at the floor.

"I'm good."

"You sure?" Adrian asked. I looked at him and nodded slowly.

"I am. I really am."

"Because if you're not-"

"If I'm not, then what? I cause a scene? I leave early? I have a fit? No, for real, I'm fine. His son is adorable. We're fine."

"Okay," Adrian said. Miles nodded slowly.

"I'm going to check on the tent. We're having dinner outside tonight."

"Oh, word?" Miles asked. "I'll come check it out with you."

"Bet. You coming, Eustace?"

"Nah. I'll be out in a little while, though."

"Cool." The duo departed. Adrian touched Ian lightly on the shoulder as he walked by the pool. Ian looked up, laughed, and resumed his conversation with Zion. Whatever they were engrossed in, their cell phones were involved. Ian pointed. Zion laughed.

I quietly grabbed the bottle of rum and poured myself another shot. I tossed it back and quickly poured another. JJ and his son came back down the stairs.

"Go on out there with Zion and Ian, Three Jay. Please." JJ asked.

"Okay daddy," Three Jay said. He ran past me through the kitchen and to the pool. I watched him interacting with the older boys, quietly at first, then laughing loudly. I looked at my drink and refused to face JJ, who I knew stood nearby.

He cleared his throat and leaned on the counter, inches away from me.

"I missed-" he began.

"He's big. Three Jay."

"He's eight."

"Eight years old. Wow."

"The girls are-"

"Five. And two. I know."

"He knows. He knows," he exhaled, mocking me. His hand brushed against mine. I recoiled. In that instant, he took my shot glass and swigged my rum. I finally looked at him.

He gulped and smiled. His eyes had a million thoughts dancing behind them.

"Goddamn," he said.

"And Syliva?" I asked.

"The good Reverend Carter is well."

"Good. Very good."

"She said hello."

"No, she didn't."

"You're right. She didn't."

"You...you, sir." I put my finger in the air, closed my eyes, and shook my head.

"Me? What?"

"You...you're here." I smirked. He licked his lips and smiled wide, baring all his teeth.

"I am here. Here I am." I shook my head and began to walk away. I felt a tug at my cargo shorts. He'd grabbed me by the back pocket.

"Here I am," he repeated. I took his fingers in my hand and removed them from my pocket.

"We should go to dinner now." I dropped his hand.

"We should." He followed me out the back door, past the swimming pool, and down the stone pathway to the beach.

"Reminds me of Curacao," he remarked.

"A bit." I thought back to one of the best days of my life.

The stone pathway ended abruptly with the white tent where dinner was served. Adrian had arranged for a long table, large enough to seat all seven of us, with an all-white and crystal décor, from crystal goblets to transparent candle holders.

"Dinner tonight will be a Bajan feast," Adrian explained. "A little bit of the best of everything here. Cou cou and flying fish. Rice and peas. Salt bread. A little breadfruit. Chicken curry. And Bajan black cake for dessert. Rum punch for those of legal age, and fruit punch for everyone else. Enjoy dinner, my brothers."

Ian sat in his chair with a wide grin as every dish was listed.

"Oh, we eatin' good tonight," he said to no one in particular. Miles laughed so hard the whites of his eyes disappeared.

"Eustace, are you starving this man at home?" he laughed.

"Ian eats good!" I declared. "Practically eats me out of house and home."

"Told you that's your son," Adrian said. We laughed.

The servers came from the house with the first course of the evening.

"Ian, it's been a while," JJ began. "Tell me again what you're doing these days?"

"Oh, I'm getting ready to go to pharmacy school," he said.

"Getting ready..." JJ repeated.

"Yep," Ian said. "When I got terminated last summer, Brother Eustace was kind about letting me stay on at his place while I got my shit together. Stuff, I mean." He glanced at Three Jay, who had ignored his slip of the tongue.

"So you're not working right now?" JJ asked.

"His job is to make sure my life is in order when I travel, which is all the time. That, and apply to grad school. And he made it in."

"Where?" Miles asked.

"Long Island University in Brooklyn," Ian said.

"Sounds like you'll be continuing with the Eustace Dailey hook-up," JJ concluded.

"That's not it at all. I wanted to stay in New York, and-"

"And he is welcome to stay with me for as long as he wants," I added, now irritated by what JJ was driving at.

"Touchy! I don't hear from the brother these days aside from social media, and it seems to me like he's living like a young socialite," JJ said.

"And didn't we all when we were 23?" Adrian said with a laugh. "I'm sure Zion's life will be similar, as will Three Jay's. Our young and reckless years are always the best years."

JJ laughed and sipped his rum punch.

"My apologies, Ian. I wasn't trying to offend," JJ said.

"No offense taken," Ian said.

"You planning on any more kids with your wife?" Miles interjected.

JJ was visibly taken aback. I glanced at Miles and lightly shook my head.

"Three is good for me. I got my ace. I got my princesses. I couldn't ask for more. What about you and Dr. Carly?"

"We're childfree," Miles said.

"Yeah, I know you don't have kids, but do you want any?" JJ asked.

"We don't want children. We're childfree, not childless," Miles explained.

"Oh. Forever?" JJ asked. Miles shook his head.

"We're not interested."

"I can dig that," Adrian said.

"Team Only Child. Know us!" Zion blurted out.

"I wouldn't have minded another child. But it wasn't a priority for us. One doesn't know the meaning of the word 'busy' until you're in the professional sports world," Adrian continued.

"But never? You're still young," JJ said.

"Yeah, we are. And Isaiah and I thought about adoption. We discussed it with Zion, and he's good with that. But if we do it, it won't be until after Isaiah retires."

JJ nodded.

"I see. Ian, you ain't got no kids stashed away nowhere, do you?"

"Nope, not that I know about! Kids will be a long ways away. Trying to get this PharmD before I even think about settling down."

"That's a good plan. It will come when it comes."

"What about you, Eustace?" Ian asked me.

"Me? Kids? Nah. I don't think so."

"Your lifestyle would change dramatically," Adrian offered.

"I know. And I like things the way they are."

"Ain't nothing wrong with discretionary income and free time," JJ said. I laughed.

The food and drinks kept flowing and our conversation loosened up considerably. We had many years to catch up on between us, and in many ways, we needed to get to know one another again. The parents. The working professionals. The wealthy young black men who were changing the world.

After the black cake was served and devoured, Zion took Three Jay inside to play video games on the big screen television in his room. The sun had long since set behind us. Lights in the distance on Mullins Bay peppered the coast line.

"I'm going to the beach," JJ announced.

"Cool, there are chairs down there if you want to relax. Nothing much to see, though." Adrian said.

"I'll come, if you want company," I offered. JJ smirked.

"I do," he said. I stood up as Ian, Miles, and Adrian stole cautious glances at one another.

"See you guys later," Adrian said. JJ nodded. I sheepishly waved and walked toward the beach.

"Hold on a sec," JJ said. He grabbed my shoulder and steadied himself after he removed one shoe, then another.

"I guess I should do the same." I followed suit, holding my shoes in my hand as we walked toward the beach chairs. The cool sand beneath my feet became smoother and flatter the closer we got to the chairs.

"Look up," JJ said. I did, and saw the nearly-full moon above us.

"It's so clear," I mused. Our chairs were close to the water and not far away from the property's edge. I sat and leaned back in the chair, staring off into the black ocean.

JJ stood over me. The faint glow from the villa's light caused an aura to form around him.

"Sit down, you're making me nervous." He complied.

"I don't want to make you nervous," he said. We sat in silence for a very long time. The oceans rhythms lulled me into a trance. My chest rose and fell. I listened to JJ's breath.

Me and him.

Him and me.

Eleven years.

An hour of silence passed.

"Is this what we're going to do?" JJ asked me.

"What do you mean?" I asked.

"Sit here like nothing happened. Like...like we didn't fall out and not speak to each other for a decade."

I turned sharply.

"We didn't have a falling out. You got married."

He turned back to me.

"All things considered...I thought you'd wait for me."

All the rage of the years welled up in me and came out in an instant.

"I waited for you, JJ! I've been waiting for you all my life. You laid there in my bed in Curacao and you told me you loved me but you weren't ready. I waited for you then. I waited and waited until you fucking proposed to Sylvia—right in front of me. And then you had the nerve to invite me to your wedding—I waited."

"Oh, you waited? You waited for me so patiently that you fucking ran away to New Mexico to get away from me! You ran away, Eustace! You ran from what we had. You *ran*! What the fuck am I supposed to do about that?"

"You go home and fuck your wife, that's what you do. You love her and you fuck her and you have the happy life you always wanted."

JJ rose from the chair and walked out onto the beach until his toes touched the water. He shouted at me.

"I *did* want a happy life. I wanted the wife and the kids and the job and the car. I wanted those things. Anybody would want those things. And Sylvia was ready for that."

"Obviously!" I shouted back at him. I rose and walked toward him until I felt the dry sand become wet.

"Well!"

"Yeah, well what? You got all those things and what do I have? I was patient. Somehow, deep inside, I thought JJ, my best friend in the whole fucking world, was gonna wake up and realize the mistake he was making. Somehow I thought we were gonna have that perfect love story that every little gay boy in America wants. I was supposed to win. I was supposed to get the guy. I was supposed to slay the dragon lady. But she won, JJ. She won, she got you, she has the kids—she fucking has it all like she always does. And you have the fucking audacity to say I didn't wait for you? I waited for you. I'm still waiting for you. I'm just waiting someplace where you can't hurt me by flaunting all this shit in my face."

"Eustace, I love you,"

"Don't...you...dare! Don't you even fucking dare talk to me about love."

I turned away from JJ and walked down the shore in the darkness.

"Come back here," JJ yelled.

"Fuck you!" I said. I heard JJ's footsteps close behind me. He grabbed my arm and I turned sharply toward him. My elbow hit his face and he stumbled backward into the sand.

"Motherfucker! You hit me!" he said.

"You grabbed me! I don't like that shit."

"You petty ass motherfucker!" he shouted at me.

"Fuck you, too!"

"Walk away, like you always do."

I turned back around and continued away from him.

"I cried for the whole weekend," he said.

I stopped walking.

"What?" I asked.

"When you went to New Mexico. I cried. The whole weekend. I locked myself in my apartment and I cried. I couldn't tell anybody why. But you know why. You're the only person I could talk to about you, but you left. And I had nobody."

"You had Sylvia."

"Sylvia's not you! She's never been you. She's not meant to be you, and you're not meant to be her. It's apples and oranges. Always has been."

"You want it all, don't you?"

"It's not like that."

"Yes, it is. You wanted me and her. Somehow you thought it would be okay to love us both."

"I did."

"And now?"

"It doesn't matter. You don't love me."

"Goddamn it, JJ."

I walked toward him and sat next to him in the sand.

"You know I never stopped loving you," I admitted.

"Then why'd you leave?"

"I got into grad school."

"Bullshit."

"...and because I couldn't see you marry her."

"You thought I was making a huge mistake," he sighed.

I swallowed hard and nodded.

"Maybe I did," JJ admitted.

"Your son's not a mistake," I quickly said.

"I know. He's the love of my life. So are my girls. I don't know what I'd do without them."

"How did we get here?" I asked after the ocean lulled us back into calm.

"Being young and dumb eleven years ago instead of following our hearts."

"Yeah, I guess so. How's your face?"

"Sore, nigga. With your aggressive ass," JJ chuckled.

"I'm sorry."

"It's cool. What do I-"

"You *know* we can't do this, right?"

"Eustace, we have to. I'm tired of living my life without my best friend."

"You can't have what it is you really want. You have too much to lose now."

"I can't be married to her anymore."

"That doesn't have anything to do with me."

"It has everything to do with you. I need to make it right. I need to make you and me right."

His body rose and fell in the moonlight. I wiped the sweat from my brow. He leaned his head on my shoulder. We sat in silence for moments on top of moments.

"JJ..." I said, slicing through our precious peace.

"Yes, Eustace?"

"I'm sorry. For all the years. For all the distance."

"I understand."

"I just-"

"Please. Don't apologize. I understand."

I stared into the dark. Waves lapped nearby.

"It's interesting. Hearing who you've become over the years," I said.

"Oh?"

"Mmm-hmm. You're a real lawyer and shit. A father." I sighed. "A husband. Power moves. Everything you ever wanted in life, really. It's what you wanted. And I wasn't there for any of it."

"No. You weren't. But I wasn't there for you, either. Look at everything-"

"I just take pictures," I said. He lifted his head from my shoulder and scooted over in the sand.

"When will you stop downplaying your excellence? Don't you know you're the dopest person I know?"

"Maybe. Maybe I was, once. But who am I now?" I asked.

"What?"

"Who...am...I...now? Who am I eleven years later? You don't know how low I was, back then. When you last saw me. I was drinking way too much. And I was feeling anxious. Every day. You know, we never...we, we...we talk about mental health as this abstract thing that doesn't impact us directly, right? It's either you're crazy or you're not crazy and we presume most of us aren't crazy. But me...I was depressed. JJ, I was in bad shape. And I don't understand. I can't understand how I could be as bad off as I was and love you as much as I did, at the same time."

"You really loved me?"

"Of course I did. Of course I did. Of course I did," I whispered. "But I ran away. We both did, didn't we?"

I hoped that the darkness concealed the tears rolling down my face.

"We were so young," JJ said.

"We were young. But we were grown. Making grown-man decisions and grown-man moves."

"I wasn't. Not the moves I should have been making."

"You have regrets?"

"One: That I didn't fight for you." His voice shook. The waves crashed onto the beach. Laughter echoed from the hills and blended into the late-night roar of water hitting land.

"I thought I was loving you more by letting you leave," he reasoned.

Silence amid the water.

"You did a selfless thing." I nodded in the darkness.

"I should have done the selfish thing."

I reached out to him in the dark. My hand brushed against his hairy forearm. My fingers walked down to his hand and I clasped it.

"We both did the right thing," I said.

"Maybe you did. You asked who you are now. Who you are now kills me. You're not the same person. Not at all. You're far greater than the person you were. I am immensely proud of you. But it kills me because you could have never been this person had you stayed. Which means you could have never been this person if you were with me."

"If you were with me, you'd never have that beautiful son back there."

"And I wouldn't trade him for anything. Truly. But no matter the kids, no matter the big house, the Beemer, the prestige. It doesn't erase the fact that I miss you. Dear God, Eustace. I miss you so much I can't take it anymore."

JJ stood up and kept holding my hand. I joined him. My feet planted firmly in the sand, he held me around my waist and pulled me close to him. He buried his head in my chest and wept. My own tears fell on the top of his head.

"I missed you, too," I said. Seconds turned into minutes and we remained joined at the chest. Finally, I peeled myself away from him.

"So now what?" I asked, sniffling and wiping away the tears.

"I wasn't sure. But now I am," he smiled through his tears. I looked at him, puzzled.

"What do you mean?"

"I'm going to do right by you in every way imaginable. I'm going to love you. And I'm going to earn you. Because this time, Eustace, I ain't letting you go. No matter what."

He pulled me back into his embrace. I closed my eyes and let myself get swept into the sounds of the ocean. I touched him, smelled him, gripped his body—he felt the same and smelled the same.

It was like being home again.

"Come upstairs," he said.

"Okay." We grabbed our shoes and headed back into the villa. The caterers had cleared everything out, leaving the kitchen in pristine condition. The dining room was bare. I could hear by the low rumbling down the hall that Miles and Adrian were enjoying a deep conversation.

"What time is it?" I whispered.

"Like two o'clock," he said.

"Damn. It's late."

"It is." He grabbed my hand and slowly led me up the stairs. We walked past Ian's room, where the door was slightly ajar. He slept on his back with his mouth agape.

We walked past Zion's room, where the door was shut and we could feel the cool air blasting from beneath the passageway.

And we walked past JJ's room, where we stopped.

"Wait a second," he said, releasing my hand. He opened the door to his room. Three Jay slept soundly in one of two twin beds. He pulled the covers around his son's shoulders and kissed him on the forehead. He walked back toward me as I waited in the hallway and he shut the door quietly behind him.

I grabbed his sides and pulled him toward me. I pecked him three times on his lips and let him go. I walked to my room and he followed me.

I turned the knob and opened my room door, and it was as I'd left it: tidy, clean, and devoid of my presence, save for my camera on the night stand.

He stood behind me and embraced me. His head rested between my shoulder blades. Entwining my arms with his, I relaxed and stood with him in the silence.

I walked forward, to the bed, and loosened myself from his grip. He followed. I turned around, sat on the bed, and hugged him at the waist, bringing his stomach to my cheek as I turned to the window. He cradled my head.

"It feels good to love you," he said. I looked into his face as he caressed mine.

"It feels good to be loved by you," I replied.

He gently pushed me back onto the bed and I rested on my elbows. He pulled his t-shirt off, revealing his still-fit torso. The trail leading down his stomach was fainter. He unbuckled his belt, unbuttoned his shorts, and slid them to the ground, over his thick thighs.

I slid back on the bed and took off my shorts. They fell in a heap to the ground, where I also threw my shirt. His black boxer shorts couldn't contain his erection, which poked through the opening.

"Happy to see me?" I quipped. He blushed and grabbed his crotch.

"Don't," I said. I moved his hands and held them at his sides. I pulled on the head and brought his penis all the way through the hole. I wrapped my hand around it and slowly stroked it. He closed his eyes and exhaled.

I took to my knees in front of him and kissed his manhood, my mouth watering for him. I put him inside my mouth and took him in as deeply as I could, until I heard him whimper. He grabbed my short afro hard.

"Jesus," he called out. I bobbed my head back and forth on his shaft and caressed his buttocks. He moved his hips in rhythm with me.

Moments later, I released my hold on him with a pop. I caught my breath, stood up, and kissed him with my hot, wetter-than-ever mouth. He grabbed the back of my neck and held me tight.

"Do you have...protection?" he whispered.

I released him, stared into his beautiful face, and smiled. I walked around the bed to my nightstand. Underneath was my camera bag. In one of the compartments were the prize: condoms and a small tube of lube.

"Always," I answered, displaying a condom. He smiled and covered his face with his hands. He pulled his underwear to the floor, and I put the condoms and lube on the nightstand, pulling down my underwear shortly thereafter.

"You look...great. Still," he said with a smile. He placed his knee on the bed and crawled under the covers.

"So do you." We shuffled over to each other until we met in the center of the bed and wrapped our arms and legs around each other.

"I can't believe we're here again," he said with a smirk. I smiled, laughed, and kissed the tip of his nose.

"We've never done things the easy way, have we?"

He laughed, then got serious. He looked at my lips, closed his eyes, and leaned in.

We kissed. We made love to each other. We fucked each other. And finally, we fell asleep in the same position in which we began: face to face, arm in arm, leg in leg, our chests rising and falling in identical rhythm.

I briefly woke to a loud knock at the door. My clock said 8:00am.

"Yo, Eustace! You in there?" Ian asked. I struggled to answer. JJ stirred, then got up and put his underwear on. His bare feet tapped the wooden floor. I turned back over in bed and closed my eyes. He opened the door slightly.

"Eu—oh, JJ. Hi."

"Good morning," JJ said groggily.

"Hey, so...is Eustace coming on the tour of the caves this morning?"

"Tour? Nah, we not going."

"Oh. Okay...so...can Three Jay come, or..."

"Yeah, yeah, of course he can. Let me go fix him breakfast."

"We just ate. He was up early."

"Oh...well let me go talk to him real quick. Make sure he's good." JJ left the room. I fell back to sleep.

When I woke again, JJ was upright in bed, reading from his tablet.

"Good morning," I said.

"Ah, good morning!" he said cheerfully.

"How are you?" I asked while stretching.

"Good. You?" I nodded. "You want some mango and yogurt?"

"Sure," I said. He produced a bowl from his nightstand which was full of freshly chopped mango and plain yogurt. He had two spoons. I took the unused one and began eating.

"So, I figure I need about 18 months," he said matter-of-factly.

"For what?" I asked.

"To separate. From Sylvia."

I gave him a puzzled look.

"I mean, she always said she wanted a whole tribe. I figure I give her one last baby, you know?"

I shook my head.

"No...I don't. Are you really talking about procreating with Sylvia right now?"

"I mean, she's my wife, Eustace. She and I have certain agreements as a family. I gotta honor them, you know."

A knot formed in my stomach.

"What you were talking last night...about making things right. And doing right by me. Was all that..."

"This is part of it, man. You're not married, you don't know. These things get complicated. I've seen it time and again, men leave these relationships and these females will do and say anything to get more than their fair share in the settlement."

"I'm not..."

"Listen. I'm a corporate litigator. I make a shit ton of money compared to Sylvia. Yeah, she's at a megachurch, but she's an associate pastor. She won't be raking in the big bucks until she spins off her own shit. And that's not happening until she's at least 40. So if I separate from her now, she's going to come at me hard for alimony. But if we play it cool, wait until she's the top earner, we might be able to call it even if she keeps the house."

"So we went from 18 months to like eight to ten years?"

"You gotta trust me. I love you. This is the plan."

I rolled my eyes.

"Don't be like that," he said. "We can figure something out. But come on, you didn't think I was going to tell her I was leaving her for you as soon as I got off the plane, right? Right?"

"No. I guess not."

"See? I rock with you, Eustace. We gon' be aight."

Life drained from my face and the knot in my stomach grew. I had the urge to take a drink.

Instead, I decided to take a swim. JJ joined me as I found my way through the empty house down to the pool. I jumped in, swam to one edge, touched the wall, and swam back. My head emerged from the water and I could feel the droplets hanging from my tight coils.

"Race you?" JJ asked.

I climbed out of the pool and stood next to him as he came out of his shirt. I stared at his chest, then his neck, then his face. Seconds felt like hours. The knot inside my stomach grew.

"Ready...set...go!" he called out. We dove into the pool and swam with all our might. Under the water, I saw him, a brown bullet trailing me by inches.

I slapped the wall, turned, and headed back to the beginning. He was feet behind me. In seconds, I had won the race.

I hopped up, inhaling deeply and wiping the excess water from my hair.

"Good race," he smiled, catching his breath as he wiped his eyes. I stared at him again, forcing a smile.

"Want a drink?" he asked. I shook my head.

"I'm good." He climbed out the pool and headed over to the bar, while I swam to the other side. I floated on my back and looked up to the blue sky, hoping for something, anything to happen to make disappear the empty feeling inside that I hadn't felt in years.

That persistent feeling was there even as our villa mates returned.

"Hey guys!" I called out from poolside.

"Hey Unc'! You missed an amazing trip to the caves!" Zion called back.

"Dad!" Three Jay said as he ran to his father. "It was awesome! We saw stalactites and stalagmites!"

"Way cool!" JJ said to his son with a smile and a high five.

"What are y'all going to do now?" I asked Three Jay.

"Mr. Adrian said we're gonna chill until dinner," he said. Adrian smiled.

"Well that sounds like a plan to me!" I dried off my arms and legs and slipped into a white linen shirt and black Adidas sandals.

"Are you gonna come to the chocolate factory with us tomorrow?" Three Jay asked me.

"That depends. Will R. Kelly be there?" I asked.

"No…I don't think so."

"Then sure, I will be there. It sounds like fun."

JJ laughed and Three Jay darted away toward the beach with Zion.

"You're good with him," JJ said softly as he squeezed my shoulder. He leaned forward and gave me a kiss on the cheek. I smiled.

Then I noticed Miles, Ian, and Adrian staring.

"What?" JJ asked. "You already knew this was gonna happen."

He shrugged and walked away. Adrian gingerly approached me.

"Everything is good," I said pre-emptively.

"Okay," Adrian said. "If it works for you, it works for me."

Miles ran his tongue over the top row of his teeth while his mouth remained closed. If I had to guess, he was counting his teeth to distract himself into silence.

Meanwhile, Ian stood there, mouth slightly agape. I walked by him, placed my index finger under his chin, and pushed up until his mouth closed.

"Wouldn't want a mosquito to fly in there," I joked.

Ian shook his head and took his iPad out of his bag.

"I been meaning to show you this," he said. He opened a streaming service and played a video.

"Your neo's probate show? Again?" I asked as I walked away.

"Big bro, it's from another angle though! One of my homegirls finally uploaded it. Take a look!"

I grumbled and sat on the sofa and JJ sat next to me. Ian's friend had some pretty good skills, considering it was cell phone footage. She focused on the action, but she also had some excellent establishing shots, as well as close-ups of older members. She even had some good shots of me and of Adrian, looking at the show with pride.

"Whatcha looking at?" Three Jay asked me as he darted back in the room.

"I'm watching a probate show from Ian's chapter. Do you know what a probate is?" I asked.

"Yeah, it's like the step show the new members of Beta do when they first cross over."

"That's right," I said with a smile. "Want to come watch with us?"

"Uh huh!" Three Jay said.

"Yes," JJ said.

"I mean 'Yes!'" Three Jay corrected. JJ and I made space on the outdoor sofa and let Three Jay sit between us. He leaned back and rested on my chest as the video played on the tablet.

JJ looked at me and smiled. I smiled back. We watched ten minutes of the show when the doorbell rang.

"I'll get it," Adrian said. He walked to the foyer, where Zion had already opened the door.

"Can I help you? Wait a minute...I know you."

"My name is Julian," the voice said. I stood up and looked through the house and saw the still-tall, still-lean, now much more rich and famous hip-hop/soul/pop superstar Julian.

"Julian?!" I said.

"Eustace!" he ran across the room and threw his arms around me. His gold chains and bracelets clinked loudly in my ears as he rubbed his hands over my back.

"What are you doing here?" I asked while hugging him back.

"I was looking for you!" he said with a gleam in his eye.

"Looking for me? Why?"

"I need you, Eustace."

"I'm sorry, what?"

"I need your photography skills, man."

"Wait, wait, wait. Wait," Ian said. "Are you really Julian? Like, *the* Julian?"

"Yes, I sure am," he smiled.

"They met years ago, right when Julian was blowing up," Adrian said.

"And I was there," Miles said.

"Yeah, so was I. Have you all seen each other since then?" JJ inquired.

"I mean I've been to some concerts. And we email each other off and on," I said.

"But I been following your career this whole time. Wait a minute...you're that model guy!" Julian said, pointing to Miles.

"Miles Davis Johnson," he said, extending his hand.

"Oh my goodness, I fucking love your work! Eustace kicked off your whole career!"

"My career as a model, yes."

"Well shit, what else do you do?"

"I'm a librarian."

Julian looked at Miles blankly and slowly cocked his head to the right.

"Oh. Well okay then!"

"Would you like to have a seat, Julian?" JJ asked.

"Thank you, sir!" Julian sat on the sofa and stretched his arms out. His personality had remained consistent over the years, cooler than cool and larger than life at the same time.

"How did you know where I was?" I asked.

"Well a funny thing happened since the last time you saw me. Apparently I'm what's known as 'A-list' now. So when I saw on social media a few days ago that you were going to be enjoying Barbados this weekend, I did some research, cross referenced some posts, called a few places, narrowed down where you might be staying, and yeah, maybe I bribed a few people to give me the location."

"And this is for...what, exactly, a gig?"

"In a manner of speaking. I'm about to go on a world tour. Eight months. Europe, Asia, Australia, Africa, and back to North America. Shit, might even throw Brazil and the Caribbean in there. When this is all over, I want to put out a coffee table book. Nothing but photography of me and my band. Well, and the people. And the places. Like, I don't just want performance photos. If we in China, I want a photo shoot at the Great Wall. If we in Paris, I want to be on the Eiffel Tower. Put me on Uluru down in Australia."

"Uluru?" I asked.

"Ayer's Rock," Miles whispered.

"Oh. I see."

"Work with me, Eustace. You are the best photographer in the game and you need to be with the best tour in the world."

"Well now wait a minute...I heard about this tour. Isn't it kicking off like...soon?"

"We'll be in Johannesburg next weekend," Julian said.

"Julian! Shit, why you wait so long?"

"Well I only had the idea last week! I found you as soon as I could."

"Julian, I can't leave everything for an eight-month tour."

"Um, excuse me Mr. Julian, sir," Ian interrupted.

"Yeah?"

"I'm Ian. Ian Kenney. Eustace is my big brother. I was wondering…how much this gig pay?"

"You his agent?" Julian asked.

"Yes, I am," Ian lied.

"Three thousand a week for 32 weeks."

"Three thousand! For a MacArthur genius? Are you kidding me? He makes that much on maternity shoots alone. You askin' my man to leave *everything* for three stacks a week? Get outta here."

"Four thousand a week."

"Four thousand? Eustace can make that with his eyes closed. You asking him to leave everything for eight months, yo. Career prospects drying up. Relationships fizzling out. *Steups.*"

"Five thousand a week, then. He'd be seeing places he'd never get to see otherwise. He'd be meeting with all types of famous people, other artists, heads of state. Free hotel room. Free travel. I will throw in a per diem so he ain't gotta worry about eating or souvenirs. It's like being on vacation for eight months and he gets to publish his first book at the end. Five grand a week and that's final."

"Second book, actually," I added.

"His first one is coming out this fall," Adrian added.

"Really?" JJ and Julian asked simultaneously. Adrian nodded.

"I didn't know that," JJ said with a frown while looking at me.

"Five grand a week? We'll take it. Adrian, have Rebecca Templeton draw up the papers," Ian commanded.

"Now wait just a damn minute! I haven't said yes to anything here," I said.

"Frat…Bruh…It's Julian. This is a once in a lifetime opportunity. Take it," Ian said.

"No," JJ interrupted.

"Why not, JJ?" Ian asked.

"Because…Eustace has clients to consider. Projects are already lined up. And I think Julian needs to show some respect and some responsibility before he bogarts-"

"I don't know, this is one hell of an opportunity," Adrian interrupted.

"I know, right?" Zion chimed in. "This is Uncle Eu's job, so why not take it to the next level?"

"Uncle Eu?" Julian said with a giggle.

"Julian…I don't know, man. This is sudden. Why you ain't have a photographer already lined up?" I asked him.

"I told you, the idea came to me last week. I was in Vegas at the BET Awards and I was thinking damn, somebody should document all this. Nobody sees this behind the scenes shit. I spent my entire life grinding to reach this point and I want people to see how it all goes down. And why not start with the tour? Look man, I know I should have been thinking about this sooner, but if you know me at all, you know that's not how I roll. I just be making the music."

"I'm sure you can find someone else, though, maybe even cheaper," JJ said.

"You're right. Maybe I can. You know, I apologize for interrupting y'all's vacation. That was inconsiderate of me, and I know better."

"I'll do it," I said.

"What?!" JJ and Julian said simultaneously.

"You only live once, right? This tour…this book…this could be huge. For both of us."

JJ stormed out of the room, through the kitchen, and out the back door.

"Well, that's one 'no' vote," Julian said.

"There's no voting at all. This is my career and my decision," I said calmly.

"And you're sure?" Adrian said.

I nodded slowly.

"I'm sure."

Julian stood up.

"Welcome to the family, Eustace Dailey!"

He took me by the hand and drew me into a bear hug.

"What an eventful day this was," Miles deadpanned.

"Mr. Eustace?" Three Jay's small voice said.

"Yeah, li'l man?" I asked.

"I'm happy for you!" he smiled. I returned the smile and gave him a huge hug, picking him up and spinning him around.

"Thank you so much, Jeremy Jacob Carter, Jr." I put him back on the ground and shook his hand for good measure.

"Well, let's go, then," Julian said.

"Go? Like right now?" I asked.

"The jet's on the tarmac. I've got papers being drawn up as we speak. And then we're getting on a plane to South Africa next week. You've got things to do now."

"Wow," I said. Adrian stepped forward with a wide smile.

"So…the hurricane strikes again," he laughed, hugging me.

"Listen man, I just stand in place. The rest of the world is spinning around me." I patted his back.

"I'm so proud of you," he continued.

"Thank you. Thank you so much." Tears welled in my eyes.

"None of that," he said. "This is what you want. This is who you are. Go out there and be great. Okay?"

"I will. I love you."

"Love you more." Adrian retreated as Ian Kenney and Zion stepped forward.

"Uncle Eu," Zion said as he embraced me.

"Zion."

"I guess this means I won't be interning for you this summer," he laughed.

"Maybe not this summer," I said.

"Can you send us postcards, though?" Zion asked.

"Do people even check the mail anymore?" I asked.

"I will, for you," Zion said.

"Then I will definitely send you postcards."

"Bruh…so agents get what, like 40%, right?" Ian asked as he stepped forward.

"Ian…don't press your luck," I laughed. I hugged him tight.

"You are going to be living the life," Ian added.

"Ian, do me a favor," I asked.

"Anything, bruh."

"Stay in my apartment while you're in school. Stay there, take care of it…do what you've been doing. I just won't be home as much."

"Bruh…I'm honored. You've done so much for me. I promise I'll keep the place straight."

"And there's something else…that book needs to come out on time. So if I did break you off a little something, do you think you could manage the PR for it?"

His eyes got wide.

"You want me to promote your book?"

"Not by yourself. Let's find a firm to do the heavy lifting. I'll do what I can from overseas, but I want you to be my proxy. Adrian can help you if you have questions. And there's always Rebecca Templeton."

"Bruh. Wow."

"You can do this. I trust you. I trust all of you in this room. You're not just my brothers. You're my friends. The best friends I ever had. Even when I tried to run from you, you went out and you brought me back. I'm grateful that you did."

"You can't stay gone from us for long," Miles said as he stepped forward.

"I'll always know where home is," I said.

"Eustace, can I talk to you alone for a minute?" Miles asked.

"Zion, Ian…start packing Eustace's bag for him. Three Jay, why don't you help them? I'll go see where your dad went."

The men in my life began to disperse. Julian was standing against the wall near the foyer.

"Eustace, thank you. I'll be in the limo waiting for you. Take your time."

"No, Julian. Thank you for this opportunity. It's a life-changer."

"*You're* a life-changer. I knew that from day one. See you outside."

He walked away and I stood by Miles. As the door closed, he spoke.

"I need to tell you something," Miles said.

"What?"

"I saw a meme on Facebook a while ago. I thought it was absurd. But for the past few days, it's been popping up in my head."

"Oh yeah?"

"Yeah. The meme said 'God wouldn't bless you with somebody else's husband.'"

I inhaled sharply and slowly let the air seep through my nose.

"You probably think I'm the worst person in the world." My voice trembled.

"I'm not judging you, Eustace. You know I'm not judging you. I love you. You've done things for me that I can't even begin to repay. But I have too much respect for you to let this one slide."

"I know."

"You love him. I know you love him. But he doesn't love you back the way you need to be loved."

"But...he does his best."

"His best will never be good enough. If you look deep enough into your own heart, you know that it's true."

I paused and looked to the floor.

"No, come here," Miles said. He stepped into my personal space and took me by the arms.

"Look at me," he demanded. I looked into his beautiful brown eyes. "You are more than this. You are better than this. The universe is making things happen for you."

I broke down into heaving sobs and collapsed into Miles' arms.

JJ had been there for the most pivotal moments in my young adult life. But deep down, when I looked, I knew that he was all wrong for me.

He was all the things I wanted to be: confident, charismatic, and a little dangerous. His reputation preceded him. His name carried respect in the streets. He was relentless. He was audacious.

And he wanted me. Good lord, he wanted me.

But he never wanted me enough to choose me unconditionally.

He was somebody else's man. He always was. He always would be.

"I love you, Miles."

"I love you, too, Big Brother." He kissed me on the forehead.

"This is not goodbye. Carly and I will see you at one of these tour dates. I promise. She loves international travel."

"I'm holding you to that." I wiped tears from my eyes.

"I'm going to see if they need help upstairs, okay?"

"Okay," I sniffed. "I've got one more goodbye to say."

Miles nodded and quickly left, bounding up the stairs. I took a deep breath and walked outside, past the pool and to the beach. JJ and Adrian were arguing.

"...you've got what you've got at home," Adrian said.

"Like you've never stepped out on Isaiah, you fucking hypocrite."

"I didn't!"

"But you wish you had. You watch your mouth Adrian. I know where the bodies are buried."

"Fuck you," Adrian said as he walked away without so much as even a glance toward me. I took another deep breath and walked toward JJ.

"Hey," I said.

"So here we go again," JJ snapped.

"JJ, please, it's-"

"Shut up."

"What?"

"Shut up and listen. Every time we get close to an understanding and a foundation for a future, you run away. *You* run away. So go. Go with Julian. And if you think this is just about a job for Julian, then you a damn fool."

"I don't know what to say to you."

"You don't have to say anything. You made your choice."

"Like how you made your choice when you married Sylvia, right? Like how you decided to have three kids with her, right? Those are the choices you made. What have I done other than live *my* life? Hmm? I lived my life when you decided not to be part of it."

"I'm glad. Continue doing that."

"I will."

"I don't want to talk to you anymore."

"You don't want to talk to me? Last night you said you wanted to figure out how to make things right between us."

"I said that presuming you would want the same thing. Eustace, I want to be with you but every time we get close, you run away. I'm not chasing you."

"I'm not running. I'm doing a job. The job of my life. I won't be locked away as your side piece to be taken out when it's convenient for you."

"Then go. Do your job. Enjoy yourself. But what we got? Forget we ever had it."

"I won't. I won't ever forget what we had. And some part of me will always wonder what we could have had if I was more patient. If I decided to be the man-in-waiting. Or if I had decided to be more aggressive. If I had decided to object to your wedding. But those things aren't in me. I'm attracted to you because of who you are. And who you are is a whole lot of things that I'm not. And that's not a bad thing. But you have to respect who I am, too. And deep down, I'm not sure that you do."

"But I *love* you," he spat.

"I know. But I don't think you respect me any more than you respect Sylvia. And as much as I despise her, how can I be mad at her? She's married to a man who loves somebody else. And yet, she stays. She stays."

JJ turned to face me.

"I'm bisexual. I'm not gay and I've never been gay. I love having sex with her just as much as I love having sex with you, or any other man I've had sex with over the past ten years. And I can assure you that you're not among the best of them."

I slowly nodded.

"I see this is not going to go anywhere else."

"Go away," JJ said.

"I will. And for what it's worth-"

"I said go away."

"For what it's worth...I did love you. I do love you. I will love you. And for a moment there, I really did think it was going to be Eustace Dailey and Jeremy Jacob Carter against the world."

JJ turned away from me and walked down the beach.

"Goodbye, friend," I said softly.

I walked back through the house. Everyone waited for me in the foyer.

"Where's my daddy?" Three Jay asked.

"He's on the beach going for a little walk. I've got to go, friend. Can I have a hug before I leave?" I squatted to his level and we embraced.

"I'll see you around, buddy," I said.

"Bye, Mr. Eustace! I'm going to go catch up to my dad." He dashed off.

"This is incredible!" Zion exclaimed.

"It's amazing," Adrian said.

"Bruh... you deserve this moment," Ian said.

"Thank you, frat. It's hitting me...you know what? Hell yeah, I deserve this!"

My fellas laughed with me.

"Aye bruh, you think I have a future in management though?" Ian asked.

"I think you should stick to pharmacy in the long run. You know. Just in case," Miles said.

Ian smiled.

"But on the real, are you and JJ-" Ian began.

"Ain't no me and JJ," I interrupted.

"Any more?" Ian said. I grinned.

"Any more," I repeated. Ian nodded vigorously.

"Okay, that's fine. Follow your heart, man. That's all you can do. That's all any of us can do."

"Let's load the limo," Adrian suggested. We walked through the foyer and to the limousine, where Julian occupied himself by taking selfies.

"You ready, mate?" Julian asked me.

"Ready as I'll ever be," I said.

"I'm really glad you'll be joining me," he said.

"Me, too. Seriously."

"Julian," Adrian said. "Take care of my baby bro. I hope he's everything you need in a photographer. Because he's everything we need in a brother."

My eyes watered. Adrian, Miles, Ian, and Zion surrounded me for a group hug amid many sniffles and tears. Julian captured the image for the 'Gram and captioned it #truebrotherhood.

After a final round of individual hugs and fraternal grips, Julian and I entered the limousine.

"To the airport, sir!"

"You got it, Mr. Julian!" the driver replied.

I rolled the window down and waved to my brothers until we were off the property and onto the highway. I rolled the window back up and absorbed the cool air.

"Well, Eustace, here we are," Julian said.

"Yup. Here we are!" I said excitedly.

"Are you ready for the adventure?" he asked.

"I think I am," I said. "You know, I didn't know it, but it was time to take this leap of faith. I've taken risks before, made spur of the moment decisions. But you know what? I don't feel like I'm running away from anything this time. This feels right."

"A leap of faith?" he asked.

"Yeah. That's what this is. I trust you, Julian."

"I'm glad to hear that," he said. "When we get settled in South Africa, remind me to tell you about the time I flew to the Caribbean in a private jet to pick up a man I've had a crush on for eleven years."

"What?" I said.

"Yeah…and remind me to tell you about the part where I agreed to pay him $5,000 a week so I could see him every day at work."

"Julian…holy shit."

He smiled and grabbed my hand.

The adventure of my life had just begun.

The End:
Boston
After Spring Break, 2016

We got back into Boston late Saturday night. Three Jay was so sleepy, I practically had to carry him on my back through the airport.

Sylvia wasn't one to be bothered on Saturday nights when she had service the next morning. That was her time to write and to meditate. And I didn't bother asking her to pick us up from the airport. We took an Uber back and quietly let ourselves into the house. I put Three Jay to bed and checked on my girls, who dozed quietly in their room.

I took a shower. Mechanically, I lathered my body, scrubbed, and rinsed. Sylvia was already in bed by the time I dried off and put my pajamas on.

In the morning, I rose at my usual time and went downstairs to fix lunches for the children.

Sylvia came downstairs in her robe.

"What are you doing?" she asked. I spread mustard on three slices of bread, then laid three leaves of lettuce over the bread.

"Fixing lunch for the kids," I said.

"JJ, it's Sunday. You can't be jetlagged. For heaven's sake, it's the same time zone!"

"It's Sunday?" I asked.

"Yes. Service today. Remember? I'm preaching."

"Oh. Sorry. Breakfast today. I'm sorry."

"It's okay," she said.

I got the kettle and filled it with water for Sylvia's tea. She sat at her usual spot and read from her Bible.

I pulled a cannister of oatmeal from the cabinet.

"Oh, can we have some yogurt and fruit this morning? It's easier. The girls were complaining about oatmeal all week and I don't feel like hearing their mouths today. You know one can't complain without the other."

I nodded and put the oatmeal away. I stared at the kettle, waiting for the water to boil.

"How was the trip?" she asked. I didn't look at her.

"It was fine."

"Just fine? It was Barbados, for goodness' sake! It had to have been beautiful."

"It was…nice." I struggled to find any further words.

"Did our son enjoy it?" she prodded. I nodded.

"He had a great time. He really got along well with everyone. Zion was with him."

"And that Ian Kenney?" she asked.

"He was the picture of responsibility. You had nothing to worry about."

"Well fantastic!" she said. I nodded.

"And Adrian's well? You know I don't watch his show."

"He's well. I don't think he watches his show, either," I laughed.

I opened the refrigerator and grabbed our fruit bowl. Apples, grapes, bananas, and some more. I placed the bowl on the counter top.

"And Miles?" she asked. I chopped an apple into small pieces for my youngest.

"Miles is good. I found out he and Dr. Carly aren't even trying to have children," I reported.

"It's not for everybody, that's for sure," she said.

I finished chopping the apple and then looked for a piece of fruit for Three Jay. I poked around and found a large, seemingly ripe mango. I sniffed it and was reminded of Barbados.

I sliced into it. I peeled back the first slice and saw that the interior was brown and mushy.

"This mango isn't good," I reported.

"Throw it away, then," Sylvia instructed. I briefly put the knife on the counter and stared at the rest of the mango. *Maybe there's a part of it I can save,* I thought to myself. Not to be bested by the fruit, I sliced at it another way, but it was rotten straight through. I tried again, more vigorously, but got the same result. It smelled great but was inedible.

Again I smelled the scent of mushy mango and went back to the first days of my trip.

I remembered seeing him for the first time in the flesh after so many years. His bushy hair. His scruffy beard. His strong arms that were built to hold me. His narrow waist that was meant to wind with me when the lights were out.

I remembered his touch against every inch of my skin. His three quick pecks to my lips. The weight of his hand in mine. The feel of his penis inside me.

I remembered his smell, from his cologne to his odor after we made love.

I remembered the sound of his voice, so deep, so comforting, so constant in a world where all I really needed was him. He might have seemed like a flake, but he was my rock when I needed one. I could always count on him.

I remembered his taste. He was sweet in the places one would not expect. I feasted upon him like I'd never have another meal, and his body responded as though my tongue was built for all those places.

I chopped at the mango until nothing was left.

"JJ, throw it away," Sylvia said.

I couldn't see the mango anymore. I couldn't see anything anymore. I dropped the knife and ran from the kitchen, down into our basement, where I had a television room. Sylvia refused to let me call it a man cave.

With the mango mush still dripping from my hands, I entered the room and shut the door. I stepped on a stray Lego that was never supposed to have been in this room and wailed in pain.

"Shit!" I screamed. And I sobbed.

I collapsed to the floor and released all the tears I had built up.

I cried for what could have been—what should have been. I cried because I hated myself for wishing my children had never been born. I cried because I was never the man that he wanted me to be, that he needed me to be.

I cried because I had lost my one true love, my Eustace, through nobody's fault but my own.

"Eustace," I whispered in the darkness. "I could never be what you needed."

I cried for a few more minutes. Sylvia entered.

"What's wrong?" she asked. She turned the light on and sat on the sofa.

"Nothing," I said. "I'll be okay."

"Nothing," she said. "Doesn't look like nothing."

I glared at her.

"Seems like things didn't turn out how you wanted in Barbados," she said. I looked at the floor.

"...and for that, husband, I'm sorry." She sat still for a few minutes as I stared at the wall ahead of me. When she was done sitting, she rose and headed to the door.

"We have things to do today," she added. "I'll see you upstairs when you're ready."

She turned the lights out and left the room. I heard her walk up the stairs and back to the kitchen.

I wiped my tear-streaked face with my hand, forgetting the mango juice that was on it. I laughed at myself for being such an idiot.

"Christ," I said aloud. "I'm a fucking mess."

Just ten minutes, I said to myself. *I just need ten minutes to get myself together.*

In the end, I needed five minutes. No matter how much I would miss Eustace, breakfast needed to be made and bills had to be paid. I wouldn't be leaving my wife today, and not any time soon. Not for Eustace. Not for any of the men I'd slept with through dating apps, or the many I would sleep with in the future.

In the end, I was a grown man who had made a grown man decision years ago. Eustace could fly the world if he wanted—he had nothing and no one relying on him. And truth be told, I wasn't mad at him for having his adventure.

I just wish the adventure had been with me.

OTHER WORKS
BY RASHID DARDEN

The Potomac University Series
Lazarus (2005)
Covenant (2011)
Epiphany (2012)

The Dark Nation Series
Birth of a Dark Nation (2013)

Anthology:
Time (2019)

Poetry:
The Life and Death of Savion Cortez (2011)

Rashid Darden is local to the District of Columbia and Northampton County, North Carolina.

Connect with him at
www.OldGoldSoul.com

Facebook, Instagram, Twitter, and Tumblr:
@RashidDarden

Made in the USA
Middletown, DE
22 April 2019